KU-197-351

'This is a brilliant book. Finely drawn, deceptively muscular, and pulsing with warm intelligence and wit.'

The Rover

'A miracle . . . move over Molly Bloom, Anakana Schofield has mastered the hundreds of voices that make up one person, and the negotiations, confusions, and occasional consolations that transpire among them.'

Little Star

'Schofield's richest gift is for spirited dialogue which crackles with humor and energy in this blackly funny, half mad tale . . . the most distinctive novel of its kind I've read in a decade.'

Irish Central

'Potent and fresh . . . In certain moments, we are not so far from Beckett's Molloy – Our Woman comes close to enlivening not only the political and the personal but also the human.'

San Francisco Chronicle

'One of the most vivid fictional creations to come along in years.'

Montreal Gazette

'Anakana Schofield's brilliantly bizarre debut novel follows a middle-aged woman as she rolls up her sleeves and charges into a late-in-life sexual awakening.'

Flare Magazine

'*Malarky* is an alternately beautiful, brilliant, profound, poignant and comedic work of literary fiction.'

Winnipeg Free Press

'Schofield's brilliant storytelling in *Malarky* is among the most engaging I've ever encountered.'

The Longest Chapter

'This is a funny, raunchy, moving read, written in beautiful, brave prose.'

The Next Best Book Blog

'*Malarky* is a journey beyond the limits of love, an equally sad and hilarious portrait of motherhood. *Malarky* is like nothing else, and what everything should be.'

Pickle Me This

'*Malarky* is a wacky, dead serious book, and what stands out more than anything is its freshness in a sea of same-old, same-old novels . . . has all the makings of being a big book of the year, if the hype should build. And it should.'

Telegraph Journal

'The novel is a challenging read, but for all the right reasons.'
Vancouver Sun

'I laughed, I cried . . . The immensely gifted Anakana Schofield's vivid study of a middle-aged Irish housewife's nervous breakdown has a huge heart and a fierce brain; *Malarky* is, by a wide margin, the most memorable fiction I've read this year.'
Georgia Straight

'With great aplomb and shite-smeared wellies, *Malarky* stomps squarely into the territory of Flann O'Brien, Samuel Beckett, Roddy Doyle, and Martin McDonagh . . . A smashing debut.'
Review of Contemporary Fiction

'Electrifying.'
Edmonton Journal, 'Five Favorite Reads of 2012'

'A stylish debut.'
Financial Times

'There were no shortage of Irish literary debuts out this year, but Anakana Schofield's *Malarky*, a take on contemporary Ireland, really stands out. "Our woman" is no typical Irish mammy, but a staggeringly well-drawn protagonist who is mired in grief.'
Irish Times, best books of 2013

'A refreshing rejection of the escapist fantasy that dominates much of our cultural life . . . I greatly enjoyed this novel, and I admire Schofield's ability to pull off something so difficult with charm and brio.'
Guardian

'Both blackly comic and deeply felt. There is something heroic about the desperate resilience of Our Woman, and the originality of her depiction by Schofield, that leaves an indelible trace on the reader's mind.'
Sunday Telegraph

'Brilliant . . . laced with dark wit and quirky lyricism, this is a striking portrait of a society in flux and a woman on the edge.'
Mail on Sunday

'An absolute hoot . . . told with chuckle-inducing black humour and deep-seated intelligence.'
Metro

MALARKY

ANAKANA SCHOFIELD

Leabharlanna Poiblí Chathair Baile Átha Cliath
Dublin City Public Libraries

ONEWORLD

A Oneworld book

This paperback edition published by Oneworld Publications 2014
First published in Great Britain and Australia by Oneworld Publications 2013
First published in Canada by Biblioasis 2012

Copyright © Anakana Schofield 2012

The moral right of Anakana Schofield to be identified as the
Author of this work has been asserted by her in accordance with the
Copyright, Designs and Patents Act 1988

All rights reserved
Copyright under Berne Convention
A CIP record for this title is available from the British Library

This is a work of fiction. Names, characters, places, and incidents
either are the product of the author's imagination or are used
fictitiously, and any resemblance to actual persons, living or dead,
businesses, companies, events or locales is entirely coincidental.

ISBN 978-1-78074-359-2
eBook ISBN: 978-1-78074-271-7

Text design, typesetting and eBook by Tetragon, London

Printed and bound in Denmark by Nørhaven

Oneworld Publications
10 Bloomsbury Street
London WC1B 3SR
www.oneworld-publications.com

Stay up to date with the latest books,
special offers, and exclusive content from
Oneworld with our monthly newsletter

Sign up on our website
www.oneworld-publications.com

For Jeremy Isao and Cúán Isamu with love

For Hannah, Niamh, Cathy, Edel & Clare with thanks

EPISODE 1

—There's no way round it, I'm finding it very hard to be a widow, I told Grief, the counsellor woman, that Tuesday morning.

—Are you missing your husband a great deal?

—Not especially. I miss the routine of his demands it's true, but I am plagued day and night with thoughts I'd rather be without.

—Are you afraid to be in the house alone?

—Indeed I am.

—Are you afraid someone's going to come in and attack you?

—Indeed I am not.

—And these thoughts, do they come when you are having problems falling asleep?

—No, I said, they are with me from the first sup of tea I take to this very minute, since three days after my husband was taken.

—Tell me about these thoughts?

—You're sure you want to know?

—I've heard it all, she insisted, there is nothing you can say that will surprise me.

I, disbelieving, asked again. You're sure now?

—Absolutely.

—Men, I said. Naked men. At each other all the time, all day long. I can't get it out of my head.

—Well now, she said and fell silent.

She had to have been asking the Almighty for help, until finally she admitted she could think of no explanation and her recommendation was to scrub the kitchen floor very vigorously and see would a bit of distraction help.

—Pay attention to the floor and mebbe they'll stop.

I recognized the potential a widow has to frighten people. I had frightened the poor woman something rotten.

The next week I returned.

—I have scrubbed the floor every day and I am still plagued by them.

Grief was silent another good while.

She had to be honest, she'd never come across a woman who'd experienced this. Usually a woman simply missed her husband without this interference.

—Are you turning to your faith?

—Oh God I am.

The two of us would now pray for some guidance because she was at a loss.

—Were they still the same images?

—Worse, I said. Even more of them and at filthy stuff together and now they all seem to be bald regardless of their ages. Did she think the devil might target widows?

—He might, Grief said. He very well might.

—Would it be worth looking into them Nigerian preachers, the black fellas I seen on the telly who can exorcise them from the place?

—It might, she said, it very well might.

*

The girls in my gang asked why wasn't I going to the grief counselling any more.

—There's something awful morbid about her. She's the sort who'd nearly put you off being alive.

And we all laughed about it, until Joanie said be careful now I think that's so and so, who's married to so and so's brother, who's Patsy's cousin and we'd never hear the end of it if it was to get back to her.

—It's awful complicated being a widow, you've to be awful careful what you say, I told them, as I'll tell you all now. If you are a widow, be careful what you say. I think it's why they started talking about Jimmy in the bank.

Mebbe I said too much.

*

In the corner of Joanie's kitchen, atop her pine table, a helicopter wobbled on a muted television, with the Afghan mountains and the Afghan mist behind it. Something of the gherkin in its green machine shape: a bulging and inaccurate feel to it.

Since the war ended, no one asked much about Jimmy, assuming him, as Our Woman had, returned to The States, until one Friday morning, a handsome postcard arrived via a German military base informing her he'd been redeployed. Afghanistan this time. She recalled the morning well: it was the same Friday Joanie suggested she apply for Meals on Wheels and she'd been angered on both counts. She had not told the girls the news of Jimmy's redeployment, fearing it would only endorse what they might be hearing in the bank, but still she found the coincidence of it appalling. All out to get me while I'm weak. I wouldn't tell them a thing, it'll only be the start of something.

"Something" was suggestion: Our Woman cannot abide them. Impertinent, ill thought out, like flipping an egg before it was ready or pulling a loaf from the oven with the yeast still stretchy and wet. Get the facts, get the facts before you come at me, she wanted to sweep them all back. That a broom could hold back a population, what a grand prospect.

Gentle and all as Joanie had been about the Meals on Wheels, it had stung her hard. With her diabetes, sure she could qualify for them, did she know? And sixty, sure young as it was and indeed it was young, was as good an age as any to apply.

It was the diabetes.

The gang didn't like the diabetes because she could no longer partake in the thick slices of fruitcake they all ate together. Will you ever be shut of it? Does it go away? The girls had asked, replacing the lid on the cake tin with a deliberate, let down rattle. Any small change to their routine created a shudder and produced the very thing she despised: a volley of suggestions delivered to deafen her with their irritation.

And down she'd go.

Concertina'd, her brain sunk to her ankles for a full twenty-four hours, how those suggestions ate away at her when she might be beating an egg or straightening a cushion. Incessantly she examined them for hidden meaning and intimation. Did they think her older than them? Would they say it if she still had a husband? Did they think her hopeless because she was a widow? She discounted that one, there were two other widows in the group, but the other widows were still dancing and she was not. I loathe the dancing. I loathe the look of those swaying couples and the heat and the hair and the smell of the smoke afterwards. Nothing would tempt me back to it. I won't go back. But the Meals on Wheels: wasn't that now the sort of thing infirm, incontinent people needed? She must get her hair done. She'd get her hair done and that'd settle it. The girls would talk of her hair and leave the diabetes alone.

*

Another worry. Maybe they'd figured out Jimmy. She must keep close to Patsy and her son, for it was at Patsy any leak would begin.

*

In response to this burst of punitive anxiety, she told the gang she was busy the next two days. An unusual move to startle them, for not a day passed that several of them didn't meet. They were like tight ligaments in each other's life, contracting, extending and sustaining the muscle of each other, house to house, tongue to ear.

The first afternoon without them she took on elaborate baking projects that mostly resulted in failure, making her feel steadily worse. A collapsed, rough-looking spanakopita sent her plunging to a new low. The spinach was climbing outside the cratered pastry, diligently clawing its way up and over the pan, while the feta cheese swum for its life at the sides. A sunken, hopeless mess. The sugar-free fruitcake came out squashed and flat as a cricket bat, as she puzzled over which ingredient exactly she had misread or misplaced. Baking powder was the culprit. It tasted worse than it appeared. The phone rang while she was outside offering these tasteless morsels to the chickens.

Let it ring, let them wonder. She took time to slowly wind back down the garden with the bucket empty, pausing to unhook her boots, customarily bash them together and position them by the mat. She would be busy for another day. The suggestions had just nudged her again. Nipped the bottom of her brain, sent a twitch down her spine into her arms, and created that unsettled feeling in her stomach of having missed a step on the stairs, that indicated the return of the thought that was never far from her all these years: would Patsy's son have said something to someone about Jimmy? It worried her a great deal more than her son being in a war zone.

Monday, she'd talk to the girls on Monday. Monday, she'd be ready again.

*

Mondays were difficult for other reasons.

Her mind stretched back to remember last Monday and thoughts of that man's stubbly neck still provoked her. A farmer he was, sure who else were you likely to find standing in the Co-op submerged in thoughts over bags of feed. Stood like a post he was in the third aisle beside the shelf that held the goat harnesses, beside the check red, warm shirts hanging up on the back wall.

—Is that shirt neck size sixteen? He had called to her, waving a shirt. She was glad the aisle was wide enough to accommodate the smothering smell of him.

—I'm looking for a sixteen. Is it sixteen? I can't read the sizes. I've no glasses.

He leaned over to her, opening his mouth for air and she spied cornflakes in there amid his mouthy parts of minimal teeth and expansive gums. The ingrained grey stubble on his face and the hostile reek of silage from his boots below gave him an air like an old jug. She marvelled that the man could leave the house in such a state, whilst softened by his need for help. His request to her, pulling her closer to the end of the aisle, bringing her into a corner she would normally have drawn her tummy in and passed. His jumper, torn at the neck, had collected and displayed much of his farming during the past week. He had a warm face, she noted. A warm face made an amount of difference to what came below the neck. No matter the proximity she might live to him, they were of slightly different worlds, hers was a more insulated union of floral curtains, the odd ornament, a framed photo and cleanly, swept fireplace, while she could imagine his Spartan bathroom arrangement, the wellies sat beneath the table and perhaps a pan and brush laid against the far kitchen wall. She could see him and his brother sat at the kitchen table eating bread and butter, slurping milky tea, not saying much, if anything at all. She ceased thinking on his domestic arrangements for she felt herself grow itchy. Yet in those few minutes of rummaging for a shirt and him taking advantage of having her attention long enough to ask carefully where had she driven in from today, she felt useful.

Hours later though, back at home, the interaction perturbed her. She worried hard: did she hand him a neck size fourteen? She strained to visualize the number on the label. She couldn't recall. He might never make the journey back to change it and would be stuck wearing the shirt with a neck too tight. Would his brother mock him silently behind the milky tea, knowing he was after buying a shirt too small, maybe too smug to tell him? Would he go into Mass squeezed into it?

At the peak of this anxiety, the day was ruined, utterly ruined and she saw no choice but to drive all the necessary miles back again and discreetly count the shirts. Might she, if she counted them, be able to find how many were missing and then know what size she'd given him?

*

Behind the Co-op, amid the cars collecting feed and fluke, she struggled to find a place to park. She entered the shop, happy to see the young fella engrossed at the counter with two men measuring chains. There was one less shirt neck size fourteen when she looked. She hung around the back aisle 'til the men buying chain were gone. She approached the counter and confessed to the young fella, who had been in school with her Jimmy some years back.

—I made a mistake, she said, I feel awful. I've given him the wrong size.

—Now if that's the worst thing ever happens to him, he'll have a good life. The young fella laughed lightly before noticing she was serious. He tapped into the computer, don't worry your head about it, I have it here, it was a size sixteen your man bought.

He came around from the back of the counter, took the two shirts from her.

—You're very good to come up and check, but next time phone and save yourself the journey, he said gently, walking her over to the door with his arm on her back.

—How's Jimmy? He asked as she stepped out past him.

—Still away.

—Must be awful hard. Where is he at now?

—Afghanistan it is now, she said quietly.

—Must be awful hard, he repeated.

On the few steps back to the car, she lifted her hand and waved at a neighbour who was struggling to get a final sack of cattle meal (suckler nuts) into an already full car boot. It wasn't true that young fellas were all drunkards, car thieves, and vandals the way the newspapers claimed they were in every other headline. That young fella's remarking was the most comfort she'd had in as many days. When she lowered the handbrake the awful thought struck her that the young fella inside might only have asked about Jimmy because he was one of them homosexuals too. The small comfort evaporated and she remembered that Joanie had said after watching Elton John on the *Late, Late Show* that she noticed gays asked a lot of questions. Joanie had said it twice. She remembered it well because she'd wanted to move on from it after the first time, thinking it ridiculous that whomever you laid down beside might prompt the number of questions you asked. But the thought was back at her now. Was he one who asked questions, that fella? Or was he genuine? She knew his mother, now she'd have to call into her someday in search of the answer.

Maybe the mother asked plenty questions too. She'd see. Suggestion, the pain of suggestion was at her again.

*

The phone rang its encore as she put kettle to cooker. She lifted the receiver to hear Kathleen.

—You weren't down to us today, Kathleen began, and I worried about you. What's wrong? Is it the diabetes?

—No, not sick, just busy the next few days, her, reassuring back, while giving no clue to what might have her so engaged. The phone continued to ring, each of the five of them. Until finally when she considered not lifting the phone it rang the sixth time and she heard Joanie again.

—Had she seen the television? Joanie wondered, the way people can wonder without explanation or making an inquiry. A helicopter with sixteen of them, I thought of Jimmy and I said I'd better ring to be sure where he is.

—It's not Afghanistan he's at, she stated. It's Iraq, isn't it?

—No it is. He was redeployed there.

—Well the Lord save us, I only hope he's not among them, Joanie blurted.

*

Our Woman added the number sixteen to the bottom of the table mat where she records all the announced losses each time the radio news relayed them. A long line of numbers with a + religiously following each one.

EPISODE 2

—Mam.

Jimmy stood eyeing her.

—Mam.

He smiled slightly and she knew exactly what he was about to say.

*

She'd ignored it, the looks, the caught embraces and the horrifying teenage moment when haphazardly one afternoon she wandered up to the barn and lightly pushed the door ajar, a crack, to quietly see the shirtless outline of him. He must have been freezing, his pale body bleary and quivering, trousers at his ankles. She could make out a hand on one of his calves, the other arm wound around the back of his legs and could hear light moaning, and a gurgled aaah that gashed his breathing, while his legs rocked back and forward a bit, urging on whoever was at him below. Her gaze returned to his behind, squinted to see where fingers repeatedly squeezed it, intent on getting the last dregs out of him. She stayed with this motion, transfixed by the bold combining of hands in pulling desire and mouth bound in a thirsty filthiness of suck and thrust. They were working hard, whoever was at him.

A bit of a slobber, not unlike a thirsty cow's tongue lapping swipe at the first sight of water.

She ascertained by the hair and the shoes it was a male with its head stuck into Jimmy's middle, but never having seen anything the like of it, she left as swift as she'd arrived, shaken, shaken to the core, then disgusted and unsure what to do about it. If it was an animal, you'd put it to sleep. Or give it a kick.

Mainly she had wanted to hit him about the head and shout *these aren't the things I have planned for you.*

She did nothing. Only the washing up. Angrily.

*

An hour or two later Jimmy came in, happy, for his dinner, suggesting the wall in the barn needed a lick of paint. Had he noticed the wall while getting his ploughing? How could he concentrate on these small details amid the wave of what was happening below? He remarked on how well the pork chops tasted, and even though she longed to slap him repeatedly around his face, she found herself locked into a silence she could find no way out of. To the cooker and back she walked, lifting and replacing pan lids. She considered spitting it out at him, let him know all she'd seen, but he was tall now and she couldn't dress him down, hissing at him like you would a six-year-old.

—What do you think you'll need to paint that wall? She said finally. Shift him out of the kitchen. Think straight again.

Immediately she felt she must exhale him out of here, he must go and stay away. Yet later that night, as she lay in bed, she recalled the light and the way the two fell on each other unabashed, and she could not lose that repeated caressing motion of those hands on her son's backside.

*

—Mam.

It had been years, and by the time the day came, she was ripe for it. Off the bus from college this Friday evening, home he was to her, stood in her kitchen, looking helpful – helpful was the way Jimmy looked.

—Mam. I've something to tell ya.

A silence brewed that she swiftly interrupted. It might be his moment, but it was her moment too and she was going to have it her way.

—I know you've something to say to me, she began briskly, I've been expecting it. Indeed I've been waiting for it. It isn't blind I am. I've a good strong feeling I know what it is. So we can make this easy. I'll give you my response right now plain and simple and there'll be no need for you to say it at all.

He nodded. Nervously. Good, she liked him nervous.

—Fellas do have companions, she started.

He nodded affirmatively. Ha! She was right on the track. She wasn't born yesterday. She'd let him have it.

—Lookit, Gerry and Joseph back the road there.

Less certain. Another short nod.

—You're going to make life very difficult for yourself if you continue with it. I imagine you'll have no wife.

He agreed quietly and politely.

She delivered her verdict in sleek, clipped sentences, like ham coming off the slicing machine.

—It's not that I didn't wonder. I want one thing understood. I'll say it the once and you won't hear it from me again. If there's no way round it, don't bring it home to me here ever. I can't have it across my door. It'd kill your father. But what you do is your business, d'ya hear. You can come anytime. But just you. And if there's any of the girls having weddings or the like, you'll come with a girl. I don't care where you find her. I don't care if you've to pay her. But for your father's sake, you'll be alone or with a girl.

She paused, briefly trying not to think of two of them holding hands. The flatness of two fellas against each other or them rubbing each other made her fierce uncomfortable. She wondered could two of them be together without touching each other. Finally, after a long pause between them, her speaking.

—I'll see you get a little extra in the will on account of you spending your life alone. I'll keep an extra cow for a few years to prepare for it.

He stood, smiled, and embraced her. You're remarkable.

She brushed him off, telling him, Go way outta that, put on the kettle and make yourself useful.

Later when she was within, adding turf to the fire, he called out from the kitchen, Mam, I'm off.

She knew it then, she knew she'd lost him, she'd lost him in a whole new way and she hadn't been prepared for the foreignness of this feeling. It didn't agree with her at all.

*

Of course she worried tall that it was off to Patsy's boy he was. If there was a way to separate them, she'd build a wall for the sake of it. She'd to steady herself into the chair as it came back to her again. She pulled the cushion, the strange one with off-colour ducks on it that one of the girls had embroidered for her and now she couldn't recall who and she wanted to recall who because she wanted her mind cleared of what was rolling in to remind her of that night. It was Jimmy. All Jimmy. She couldn't blame the other boy for he was the younger. If she'd turned away she could have saved herself, but she did not. Every time she saw a cup or glass of orange squash, it would come back to her. She was in it now.

*

It's the time of the day when you cannot be sure of what you're seeing. You might see a neighbour, think him one man, and when he approaches find him to be another. I catch movement in the next field and wonder of it. No one would be in that field at this hour of the day, for my husband's beyond in the house and won't head out for another hour. Jimmy has the car. I pull close to see what's the person at over there.

It's a young fella alright, he's against the far wall where the field dips in a funny old way. He's at an angle, bent over a medium-sized boulder of stone that's embedded into the land there, the grass below eaten right under it by the goats. Something there, he has, mebbe coats it is, rolled up between his ribs and the stone. I crouch low where a length of briars there will shield me and shuffle along. Fella, he's more of a boy, for his head lifts up a few times, and I'd know that boy, it's Patsy's boy Martin, I'd nearly be sure. And I see the other boy with him, who's less of a boy and more of a young fella and I know that young fella anywhere because he's my Jimmy. Maybe Patsy's boy is stuck? Wait now 'til we see.

I've to scout along the way, tucked right down for fear they'll see me and panic, so I keep down 'til I can get a better view.

Then I see it, the bareness.

Was he going to the toilet? That would be unusual. Is that why his trousers are down? The Lord save us he'll catch his death: he's out in the rain with his trousers down. He's up to something. I don't like it. They're up to something. Hard to see. I must see. I must be sure.

*

For once she's glad of the brambles and the height of them, and that her husband never gets round to tearing them away. And God again there it is, there's the head on the bundle of jumper, it's Patsy's Martin, the boy must be two years younger than Jimmy, is he in eighth class or ninth class? But now she's his face directly in view, a face registering something, whatever Jimmy is doing, the boy doesn't shout out. She wonders if the boy, has he fallen, is Jimmy helping him? So she's back from the briars, skirts along the wall, returned to her other angle. She's to understand why are their trousers down if the fella is just stuck. She considers interrupting, but the poor face on the younger boy would take a stroke. Whatever they're at, it's taking a while. There's a bit of rustling and rummaging, a slow manoeuvring. Jimmy's hugging him with one of his hands, but the other is missing. Wherever it is, it must be below the waist.

Until no. Now it's clearer, she can see exactly what they're at: her Jimmy, the boy she raised so well, her quiet caring Jimmy moves up and down on his tiptoes and both hands are at the boy's hips, bringing himself to and fro a small bit, like he's hunting for something lost in there. One glimpse confirms it, swift but unmistakable. There it is, two sets of hips, firmly interlocked, there's only one place her son can be, he is inside that boy.

The shock takes her to a squat.

A sunken squat.

An utter of shock.

Before she moves quietly off, she takes another look. She has to see it again.

They're still at the same malarky. It's her son, her boy, and he's shaking himself stronger against that young fella. He cannot bury himself deep enough in him. Flagrant, he's got him by the hips, rattling in and out of them, almost like he's steering a wheelbarrow that's stuck on a stone, going no place.

*

Jimmy brought Patsy's boy Martin back and offered him orange squash. My hand shook making it. I watched the two of them go out, they passed the kitchen window but stopped too soon, forgetting that single pane at the end where I could still see all. Jimmy kissed him goodbye and the boy squeezed his fist into Jimmy's groin and laughed. There I have told you now. You have heard it now.

*

Oh and Patsy.

—Martin visits Jimmy often you know. I gave her the hook.

—Oh sure he's awful fond of Jimmy, says Patsy, I'm glad of it. He'll never go anywhere unless Jimmy is down. Otherwise he's inside all the time with a long face on him. Martin's clever, does ever so well at school. And boys can be such messers.

Patsy's husband, a broad-cheeked man, missing so much of his hair, nature only left a band that folds delicately across his head, entered at that point from the fields, his wind-burnt skin gave him a glow. He hadn't the dour quietness of my husband, instead he's delighted to see me, perches on the edge of a chair, stacked with towels, refusing to let his wife remove them for *not at all, he's on his way out,* and *how's she getting on* and before she can reply, he's onto Jimmy. How's Jimmy doing in Dublin?

—He's down, I said.

—Tell him to call in and see us, the father insisted. Sure Martin will be glad to see him. We'll all be glad. He's a great lad.

How intimately our boys get along. I believe I may have spotted my son inside your son yesterday. But no, he's up and out, he's cows to move and I am all thanks for the tea, you'll have another, no, you will and no, I must carry on.

I left carrying more weariness than that with which I'd arrived. Not only had my son taken advantage of a boy, but a quiet boy, with a face as long as a month of Sundays. All terrible, all told terrible. The only thing left was to be shut of Jimmy for no one would believe it. Only that I saw it, and I could barely believe it.

*

She cannot bear Jimmy to touch her. He has been up a hole that nothing should go up. Only down, down, down. He's done for. He must be gone from this country, this country where there is no forgiveness for such a thing.

EPISODE 3

The gang do not tell Our Woman that three of them are heading to the protests in Shannon.

Bina surprised them all and during the peaceful protest pulled a hammer from her handbag, charged one of the planes and gave it a few digs.

Our Woman saw her on the news.

—She never said she was going to do that.

—She did not.

—We had no idea.

The girls discussed why Bina had not told them she planned to do this.

—You'd have stopped me, Bina said.

—We would, they said.

To Our Woman, who saw the story on the news and recognized the back of Bina's coat as they took the hammer from her, they only said, we didn't tell you because we thought it would upset you what with Jimmy and the like.

—Not at all, not at all, she said quietly.

New territory. The territory of not upsetting the widow.

EPISODE 4

Get out and about a bit, my husband urged me, go in to town, have a look at the shops. I lived alone then with my husband. If you're wondering I have three children, though now I have only two and no husband neither. No matter who called in to me, the loneliness inside my kitchen and my weary head would not abate. It was strange that. Strange like someone had thrown a cup of tea at the curtains that obscured my brain.

You've had enough I could have sworn they said that one time in the hospital when the doctor gave me a jab, I was certain they were putting me down like you would an old donkey. You've had enough, we're going to let you go. But the nurse, when I looked at her, her lips weren't moving.

—Go into town and have a look at the shops. Have a bowl of soup some place. It'll do ya good.

It was the second time my husband instructed me that day. The shops, to the male, ever the solution to the glowering female, but in this instance they were no use whatsoever for unbinding me from my misery.

I could barely make out the colour of things, once inside I couldn't find my way back out to the door, I would stand and stare at pillows or lamps, immobile for so long, eventually people asked was I OK and three times offered me a drink of water and a chair. But I commend my husband, his words about the bowl of soup hung about me and didn't I take his advice and step into a place I never normally woulda gone near. The sort of place you might peer at, but you'd never have need in this lifetime to go in.

On the outside it had the look more of a pub than say a cafe, but it was the bar of a small bed and breakfast-type hotel. The woman at the bar had hair you might see on a shop dummy. Cut the same way for so long it would never change its shape. She and the place kept the form of the 1970s even though they were long gone and everything around the building had changed. They were like a tribute to it. Would you believe me if I told you, they reminded me of my wedding cake, but I sat hidden away inside there and my husband was right, it was quiet and it did me good. It did me snug, if you see what I mean.

Unfortunately, it was the reason I was so easy to find when Red the Twit came for me.

*

Our Woman lies in bed. Her skin feels as though it has been lit, beginning at the tip of her little finger, but her husband's refusal to add a spoon of gasoline means it will be a slow burn, raising every centimetre of her flesh, scorching her East to West.

She peels back through the conversation, the homily, delivered by Red the Twit earlier that day in the window of that place she entered to escape from the world. Her ear on the pillow, facing away from him, and tears dribble and drip while she thinks on it. She swallows repeatedly to avoid sniffing for she does not want the turn of him, the what's wrong with ye? Or what are you sniffing about?

You don't know me, but I must talk to you. The woman, Red's approach, inside that place she'd gone to sit and think, she remembers first. Taken unawares she was when Red struck,

watching a woman through the window on the other side of
the street with a collection box for The Hospice, entranced
by how generous the stop of people was. Then she'd felt it.
The grip of her arm: the battiness of Red's first words: *I have a
confession but before I make it, you must pray with me.* (Is that Dublin
in her accent? She's a puzzle. Red's a puzzle.)

Chipped nails (could there be anything more common on
a woman?) meshed with her forearm and she could feel the
trace of the salt pot against her wrist – not even a wriggle – the
woman had her tight. And she intoned, did Red, an adapted
version of Grace, usually delivered before sprouts or spuds, *for
what I am about to say I ask the Lord's forgiveness. Bless Philomena* – she
used Our Woman's first name – *for what she is about to hear O Lord,*
and then Our Woman became nervous, very, very nervous.

Not able to peg this apparition opposite her as a simple
head case, or a case of mistaken identity, for the Red-Nailed
Twit has used her full name and there is only one person who
could have told her. Only Our Woman's husband calls her
by her full name. Nobody since 1956 has used it, other than
him. She's been Phil, but today she's Philomena. Philomena,
Our Woman, who braces for the gush of what Red the Twit
is about to sell her.

Red began the best way, describing her communion with
God.

*Hear me out, for you'll hear how I was touched by the hand of
God, and I am here because he sent me. It was an ordinary Thursday,
I had caught the seven o'clock train from Ballina to Dublin, you know
the one that has you in town by eleven, and you've just to jog down to
Henry St and the Jervis Centre and you can have a lovely lunch or go
and visit someone in the hospital and then back down the Quays to
Heuston, the traffic is awful and the pollution catches you in the throat,
but as soon as you're on the train like you know, a cup of tea from the
cart and all's well like you know. On this day I have no idea why or
what took me that bit further down to Capel Street, I always used to be*

afraid you know, I'd get mugged or beaten if I went that far down, but something pulled me there and I can tell ya, hand on my heart, I won't tell you a lie, it was the hand of God. I was pushed by his palm. She paused, lifted the manky tea cup full of water, took a swig, and returned her hand to Our Woman's forearm. *Have you ever had that happen?*

Our Woman confirms she has not.

Well please God you will. And I walked down there, imagine, I'd never put a foot on that street in all me life, and I passed the sofa shop, nothing, and I love sofas, but nothing and on a Polish food place, Polish Skelpi . . . you know phone card posters on the window do you know the place?

Our Woman confirms again she does not know the place with Polish phone cards. Nie do Polski Skelpi.

And on and on I walked for I was worried, the anxiety lifted in me as I passed Naughty Knickers, it almost had me off me feet and there was a good reason why but I had to go on and then, at the door, it came again, try as I might I could not go past, not able, would you believe my feet would not move, I swear to Jesus it was paralysis. I began to call out, my feet, my feet, my feet will not move and people stared and one woman asked: What's wrong wit ye? But I turned to the building and saw the words Calvary Christian Centre and it was like walking inside the warmth of a hat, or the holy house on Achill. I was hot by the time I reached the door, my face flushed, I turned the handle and in I stepped. The first thing I remember is the blue doormat, blue what a strange colour for a doormat. I mean have you ever seen a blue doormat?

No, Our Woman confirmed, no blue doormat.

It was a small room, only a few wooden chairs and cheap carpet, but the bible was there and I sat into one of the wooden chairs and the voice came to me that I had to come and find you and admit. Taste and see that the Lord is good it said on the wall, and I realized the Lord was speaking to me of that what I had tasted and I must come and confess to you or I'd never be saved. And I can honestly say, and this I say for I hope it will make you feel better, I can honestly say that what I tasted did not taste good.

And she paused, which gave Our Woman opportunity to explore her face. For clues, for identity, for, well, anything. She was a woman hinging her way towards her mid forties perhaps, she had years of advantage on Our Woman, but the smokes had crinkled her. Cheapened by a floral whiff and unfortunate nails and she must excuse herself a moment to have a cigarette outside, would she, Our Woman, join her?

No, no, Our Woman speaking, I'll wait.

Our Woman remained at the table and thought, she thought hard. What news could this woman be bringing her? Why had she pinned her at this table?

And when she returned, her hand forced Our Woman's forearm back to the table where she continued to pin her. She asked questions. *Has she got a continental quilt or a clock radio?* Our Woman admitted to neither. I've an electric blanket and a dring, dring wind-up clock, why?

Well it's just on this day that I am telling you about, the day that has forced me to come and find you, I had set out with the intention to buy both, probably at Argos for they've the best prices, do you've any idea how hard it was to find you, he doesn't say much about you, he wouldn't tell me anything when I told him I had to come, he said I was a messer and I wouldn't do it and that you wouldn't believe me. But you will believe me won't you? You will or the good Lord would not have sent me to you.

For her own private reasons, Our Woman agreed yes, she would believe her. But, unusually for Our Woman, she interrupted. It wasn't her usual polite interruption, which would've been *I don't mean to cut across you but,* or *Come here to me a minute there's something I must ask you before I forget.* Our Woman was direct.

—How, she said of her husband, then how does he start? Where does he begin?

The Red-Nailed Twit lifts her right hand and indicates her left nipple.

But missing the cue, the cue to plead for forgiveness, excuse herself to the toilet, to allow Our Woman a dignified exit, Red the Twit carried on.

But . . . that didn't bother me, it was his other business. At this she passed a hand around the back of herself, maybe heading lower than her kidneys, Our Woman is not entirely sure.

The licking!

She sucked air in, an astonished respiration, and gave a cherry-giggled smile. *I've never met one of those before! A licker!* Another cherry glint in her eyes. *I thought he was doggy at first, 'til it started. At first I was shocked, but I grew used to it. And here.* She indicates her armpit. *He was always hosing me here.*

Our Woman has sunk into perplexity. She tries to visualize her husband at the back of this woman conducting himself in this manner. Our Woman examined the new exhibit before her, the crinoline armpit.

She was practical, Our Woman.

—Sorry, exactly what was he putting in your armpit?

His thing, she giggled. *His dirty thing, of course.*

Our Woman tried to calculate how it might fit: oblong, side or straight.

At first I thought he was going for me mouth . . . and I am fussy about me mouth.

Red ceased, praise the Roman soldiers she ceased. Realized from Our Woman's face that shock had been absorbed. Our Woman had begun her lift from the table, but the twit entreated her,

What I done with him was wrong – very wrong. But I want you to know it was all me, all me, not your husband. Except the first time. It was him the first time, of course it was him the first time, but every time since it was me, me, me. I want you to know the Lord has taken me in and I am working hard for him and I am atoning. I volunteer. I do the flowers and the hoovering. I wash the tea towels and I want you to do me a favour.

Our Woman offered only silence.

Would you please forgive your husband? I want you to. He doesn't deserve it. It was all me.

Mere seconds and there was a rustle. The tablecloth dragged suddenly away from Our Woman. Instinctively she lifted her hand as it pulled, to let it go, and thus the table cloth and the Red Twit flopped back, chair sideways over and to the floor. The attention of the room turned to the table because the pot of tea was all over Our Woman's lap, but the focus was on the Red-Nailed Twit, she had passed out. The eejit was out cold.

*

Quick they were to water and ambulance. She was around by the time the ambulance men arrived and answering their questions. *Yes lightheaded. No hadn't eaten. Fasting. Seventy-two hours approximately. A religious fast. No, no not Ramadan. Jesus. Our Lord.* She's a Christian.

Was Our Woman, nearby mopping her legs and skirt, a relative? No, no, Our Woman shook. Would you drive this woman home? She cannot be alone and we've to get out and handle an angina attack out Foxford way.

Trapped. Our Woman would, of course she would. God bless you Mrs, the ambulance man said putting his hand to the small of her back. You're very good. You're very good.

—I'm not a Christian, she told him.

*

Red lived in a Ballina housing estate with a faux French misspelled name. Very difficult to find. Our Woman cannot believe the cruelty: trapped in a car with a woman who has crumbled her, delivered this crushing news. Our Woman took advantage of the chance to quiz her. Where did she work? An old folks' home, with a funny name, mostly nuns. Was she married? No, she could never find anyone willing to marry her. How did she meet Himself? She'd rather not say.

Things were silent.

Will she come in for tea? Red asked.

Our Woman will not. Audacious, she thought, beyond audacious. Over the hills and far away nerve damage. As bold as life on Mars. As Red the Twit left, Our Woman hailed her back. How am I to believe what you've told me?

Listen take it easy on yerself, just forgive him.

—But if I am to forgive him, how will I know he did it?

There are items of mine in your house. He took one thing each time we met.

Red the Twit's eyes said underwear. The international language.

On the drive home from Ballina, with few street lights to facilitate her, Our Woman considered crashing the car into a wall. There was a lovely black spot of a bridge, sharp and marked with the white crucifixes and moulded flowers of the other thirty taken non-deliberately in this spot. To be found mangled in a car, head to the wall or dashboard, might be easier than excavating the mind of the man who waited beyond at her kitchen table.

*

It was another way for the girls in her gang and their husbands. Our Woman observed their lives tied up and in with their husbands in small, significant ways that hers lacked during those days of her marriage. A husband might look out for his wife or display inquiry about his wife or the one that touched her most was how they could offer to relieve a burden.

They might lift a box for you. That would be useful. She was sure she had witnessed this, but couldn't cite a clear example, with a name and set of knees attached. It must be enough that it happens.

Today with Himself gone out to the fields, she wipes the inside of a cup with a tea towel, the insulting slur of a tannin streak refusing to budge at the behest of her knuckles, while she tries again to retrieve such moments. Mostly she sees couples bickering in the upstairs cafe or between the clothing rails of Dunnes Stores. The groaning guts of those men spilling over the belts of their trousers, while handles of paper bags shackle them at the wrists. The most tenderness she can find is in teenagers, a young woman with her hand vulgarly slipped into the back pocket of a young fella. There's aggression even in the way they kiss each other so flagrantly, like they're trying to suck the other's gums out, like an old horse chasing a lost scrap of ginger nut biscuit down the palm of your hand and up your sleeve.

So she cannot name them, but she's seen these exchanges, she's certain. That such things take place will have to do.

*

And behold, here he is now, Himself, my husband, in from the field to the kitchen, pulls his chair to the table for our evening sequence. I commence my bit, quick lay of the plate afore him, and back to hover and hope. There are a series of tiny motions I await, biteen actions that if totalled indicate he's here. Daily I must ascertain this. That steam might rise from the food, register its heat, and thus celebrate my labour in making it. That he'll pull his cup toward him, a gesture of inclusion. Best, when he engages all things on the table. If he'll lift the salt, the pepper, swoosh it over the food, stamp it down and immediately up with his fork, before the dip of the chin to let the scooping begin. Oh I can watch this sequence, day beyond day, for it's only in these sole actions I know he's here with me. And I have learnt what prevails when these actions are interrupted, I've met what this leads to, that day in the bar of that bed and breakfast, when your one, Red the Twit, approached me. All this examination, all this watching, unsettles him.

—Sit down. What's wrong with you standing there?

But I am waiting, hoping for a reach, not a ride like the young ones – talking between bites of a burger at Supermacs, say. My objective is ever to avoid sitting, or passing things into his palm. Instead I must hold back to register a reach, which I'll see because the hairs on his arm become momentarily visible beneath the sleeve of his worn cardigan. Only then can I, will I, could I, would I, sit.

That day though there's no stretch: eke it a second, wait now, mebbe, but no, he's not going for the cup. He looks at me, waiting for a response. He indicates the chair opposite him. His hand willing me to sit, but that's the very hand that must circulate around the table moving objects like a game of domestic draughts. And if I sit, those objects will be passed and passing robs me of the sequence.

—I've already had mine.

The truth is, I'm filling up on the reliable aspects of my daily life that my husband, no matter what else he does, will come home to me from the fields for his dinner, he expects to find me here, and I rely on this expectation and these days I study it. I study it because I know there were days I missed it and I have to mull over those days. I am learning how to pay attention.

*

Offensive: the offensive is to have him move the objects around the table the way I like them moved. An undertaking is what I want.

*

I lift the salt and hand it towards him. To tempt the undertaking: Do you need a bit of salt mebbe? Resistance. No words. Just a wave of the auld hand and a slight shake up around the eyebrows that say *go 'way woman*. They're dismissing the salt. No, no salt.

And onto our second reliable sequence, he'll dribble out a report of what did or did not take place beyond: who had cows to be moved or the trouble he was havin' with a hose, what small repair was out of the question essential, or neither of us could carry on for a stampede of cattle would be in on top of the two of us. His voice scampers up with emphasis and insistence, like he's instructing sailors on a boat about to sink. *I can't let it go any longer, the fence is down, the cows will be in the road, the dogs will get in at the sheep with it all down and what use will they be then?* And then he mounts to the daily conclusion yes *He must head out again. Sure it's never ending, so it is.*

—It's never ending, I repeat for him.

—I don't think people have a clue how hard farmers work.

—They. Do. Not. Three separate words I give him. Why was he telling me this? Disturbing. As if I'm not here. He's here, I'm not. He's out in the fields, I'm not here in the house. I'm gone from his daily activities. Am I gone?

Every dinner concludes with him heading out again. It was one of those nights that he headed out to the fields that I lost him, so I carry on down to the gate to be certain he is where he said he'd be.

Today, though, at the table, he's still not speaking.

*

Our Woman was worried. There hadn't been enough movement. Too little mass, she needed objects on the table, if there was to be any hope of him shuffling them around.

*

If he doesn't want the salt, I must interest him in something else on the table. There's to be movement on this table this evening or so help me God I'll be forced to examine the reasons why. And I know when I start examining I'll discover all the things I hate to hear. He had his hands up and down another and his mind was away. All day I've been looking at that table and visualizing the objects with the exactitude of a cricket fan before I placed them where they sit now on the tablecloth. It was deliberate, tactical, within arm's length, at eye-catching corners. Why, why isn't he taking them? He must be at something again. He must be up to his tricks. Back up Red the Twit.

Over to the fridge – I've never liked the handle of it, too thin and chipped – where I remove two bottles of sauce, return, plonk them on the table, and uncap the one. Will he have a drop of sauce on his potatoes?

I've employed too much economy in my force, overwhelmed the table, for he knocks the vinegar over, curses as it sneaks into a puddle – bottles must be placed uncapped you see, ensuring the path of least resistance. There's the worry he'll rise soon when he must be seated, for if he's up, the sequence of talk will be broke and so I strike some of the objects. Milk, milk for the tea, milk in a jug, he'd be comforted by the jug. The blue stripy jug. He'd pick it up. Surely to God he'll pick up the jug.

No.

Not today.

Today he's utterly indifferent. Rejects the milk and cracks his fork on the plate, displacing knife to tablecloth. I manoeuvre it off. He lifts the bottle and begins reading it. Might do, will it do, it isn't primary movement, it's accidental, secondary, but it's something.

—Isn't this queer stuff? I've never understood the point of it at all.

—Will you have bread? How about a bit of bread? I have to get off the questions, they're upsetting my sequence. A slide, breadbin open, slice to table before he can refuse. Plated and I'm happy. He accepts it, tugs the plate a touch, he's going for the knife. Glory, glory be.

—Give it here to me 'til I wipe it with a warm cloth, it'll slice the butter easier.

Unity between knife and butter, I didn't want him to refuse either. Deflect him to the jam.

It's on the round table for the table is round, our only table is round, why have we a round table when a square one could accommodate more variety of bottles, but distant it is, that jar by the wall.

—Jam?

The jam, hand to jar, unlidded as swift, assumed a sudden position by his elbow before he could answer. Jam, I think, take it, take the fecker.

—Yes, yes um.

Absentmindedly, he's on the jam, upon the bread and folds it into his mouth and chomps and – yes! – the arms and hands push the jars and bottles about.

—I'll come with you, I say.

It's over to me.

The third squeeze of our sequence where I have the possibility to deliver news about what someone said today in the kitchen, either a visitor, or heard on Midwest Radio, but I foul up. Instead of introducing snippets from the locality, which would keep him at the table and aide the precious movements I've waited all day on, I move straight to being useful. These moments – moments I'm only assured of once a day, for lunch is rarely taken at the table, either on the lap or down the field – have been given the shove.

—You could stand at the gate, but you wouldn't want to get your feet cold, Himself offers.

He's obsessed with the temperature of my feet. Sometimes in bed he'll ask are they cold, and if I say they are, away he'll go, down to the bathroom and pull a towel to put over them. He never inquires of the rest of me, only the feet, the feet.

When I die, he'll keep my feet on a bookshelf or at the top of the cupboard.

There will be no standing at the gate, not at all. I'll be down lifting and moving and shifting and he knows it. If he's honest, it's poorly built for farming he is, and it's me who's the sturdier of the two of us. I could grab the mallet from him and bang a stake before he'd have the words to ask.

I've heard him remark to other fellas that *on his oath she's stronger than him or any two fellas.* He once confided his fear to me that he'd get injured, become useless, and I'd be done with him.

Today I hear the words of a guilty man, a guilty-thinking man, who within his carryon has never warmed nor warned to the realization that I am capable of the same tricks as him.

You worry too much about Jimmy, he tells me. Sometimes I catch him examining the back or side of my head; no doubt he's wondering whether my thoughts might enter the same register as his. But I've no need to examine the side of his head, it's all available to me on the table, each day in the manner he does or does not pull the cup, lift or lower the bottles, and the way he eats his dinner. I can tell everything about him from such simple movements. And the fool never grasps it.

*

Twelve hours, her eyes streamed uncontrollable, she sniffed into the dim light, the rain, the knock at the door – those eyes continued to stream, resisted it all, her tears did not desist at interruption nor embarrassment. Real tears, solid silver ones.

She stared at the sink, yellow glare on the porcelain. She wasn't sure how long she'd been there, but when she moved to the window it had turned dark. He had not come home. What a profound waste of sniffling.

Appetite gone. She could not imagine food. In her head, she tried to see a plate of potatoes and a piece of chicken, but nothing. She tried to swallow a cracker but it scraped the back of her throat and she had to spit it out.

How long could this last? Hours, hours and hours with no desire to eat, and her legs fizzy from the lack of food and her body showing every kind of sign, yet again her head would not let her eat. She would never feel hungry again. Her appetite amputated out of her brain.

Soup, sips of soup and that was it. Watery, dreadful, powdered, tomato from a clumpy packet was all she could swallow. Yet she must make his dinner.

She gave herself three days. Then it, all this, must end.

*

She lay and thought. She thought and lay. And thought some more and this was what she thought about. She thought about the fact she did not know what she was supposed to do. She'd not been trained for this. She thought about the fact she lay in a bed while her husband had lain in another bed. She thought that she could lay with the thought her life had come to this, yet this was exactly what she'd imagined it might be during those years of waiting. Her very worst picture, that, of people who live together rolling along, rolling through the century and no matter how they try or don't try, wake up decades later to the realization they'd been quietly making each other miserable. And she was surprised at how unsurprised she was.

She was miserable, but quietly accepting. She was miserable, quiet, but accepting.

Should she wail and call out? Should she go in and fight for a droopy-eyed man? A man no woman in her right mind should want. Yet there was always a woman to run to: How was that? And now what was expected of her? She understood what was required to clean her house, to clothe her children, she did not understand the version of life that had presented itself yesterday in the B&B. She didn't recognize the hat, nor face, nor fingers on it. She hadn't been trained for this. She'd been trained for marriage and funeral and baptism and weeding and shifting and turning, but not wondering. This wondering was new for her. The wondering of why she didn't understand how to wonder. She did wonder but she was not officially certain how to do the wondering. Should she wonder passively, quietly, while stuffing a chicken in the quiet enclaves of herself? Or should she wonder loudly, spewing and cajoling him for information and revelation and try to trap his fingers in a door until he'd tell her all of it? All of it was what she wanted, in all its awful sordidness, and to be awful it would need to be sordid, but she knew he'd never give her anything but the hint of it and this was what sickened her.

For a while, hard and fast tasks kept her mind occupied, angry but occupied. She brushed the floor, nearly lifting the tiles. She scrubbed the grooves between each tile fiercely 'til she saw her finger bleed at the cuticle and she let the blood go into the grooves of the tile. Now he'd find the stain of his actions underneath his feet.

Most of all, she hadn't paid attention.

She'd look at that stain and remember to pay attention.

*

The first day after Red's revelation she cut chunks from his potatoes. Knobbled them, deformed. She added salt to the butter and allowed an insect to cook with his cabbage.

The second day she omitted to place tea in the pot and when he lifted it he uttered a cry. *It's empty! There's nothing in it!* which reminded her he must have issued a cry the first time he pushed himself into Red the Twit. Perhaps he was surprised to find himself there? She wondered whether or how he would have made it in.

The fourth day she reduced the teabags inside the pot to one, and he commented the tea had gone very weak, as though it was being controlled by the weather or an outside force. He did not lift the lid of the pot, because he was not accustomed to doing such things for himself.

The fifth day she left him no dinner and caught the four o'clock bus to Dublin to visit Jimmy, her son.

EPISODE 5

With no sign of her, Himself phoned.

—She's here. Jimmy held out the phone. She shook her head.

—She's in the toilet. She'll give you a ring back. Her son lied for her, precisely how she has trained him. And when he replaced the phone asked nothing, only said I'll put on the kettle for tea and then we'll head into town.

That night Jimmy brought her out. There's no question, I'm bringin' you out, he said, proud. They caught the bus, down the quays, by Trinity, when she saw them. Pink words, neon, beaming from the wall.

—Lookit the pink light what is it? She read the words *I wouldn't give a snap of my fingers for all their learning.*

—The city is lit up with them, Jimmy said. They're all over the place.

She craned her neck across, scanned the pub roof opposite, but couldn't find the source.

—What is it? Where is it coming from?

—I dunno, Jimmy said, but it's so pretty. Jimmy dropped his head to squint the last triangular moment of it and then gone. All gone. She wanted more of it.

—There are nine of them apparently, another one by the Martello Tower. It took me weeks to notice them and now I look for them every time. We'll go tomorrow, we'll go and look for them.

—I won't go home 'til I see them all, she said quietly. The words were for her, she wouldn't give the snap of her fingers for many's the thing, *I wouldn't give a snap of my fingers for the swaying, I wouldn't give the snap of my fingers to get the skirt off Red the Twit.*

*

Jimmy already had a plan to meet the lads in town and she insisted he not cancel it.

—We'll be going to a bar mam, are you sure?

She bought knitting needles in town and started work on a jumper while he socialized with the lads. They were young, they were young lads, all of them. Their faces freshly shaved and the funny thing was the bar was full of men, there were few women. And they'd tee-shirts about them. And security guards. A few had bald heads and earrings and the like. But they were pleasant, laughed together. One slid his hand along Jimmy's forearm as he rose from the table to go to the toilet and kept his body close to him as he passed, not making the normal polite dip away to avoid his bum scraping the man's chest. She caught it, squinted away from it to her wool, and created a new box to put it in.

She continued to knit as the music grew pumpy though she could no longer hear every word of the conversation. But they were lovely to her the fellas, admired her knitting, asked her questions. One said his mam was a farmer too, asked her about headage. And what did she think of the EEC? And was Jimmy a member of Macra na Feirme? And how his father made him join it and everyone erupted at the invocation and joked about whether he'd fancied the chairman. She didn't understand every word because of the noise, so she nodded and smiled if they looked at her. Eventually they settled back into each other and forgot about her. Every now and then Jimmy asked her if she wanted another red lemonade.

The other lads headed on to a club and hugged Jimmy goodbye. She wondered was it strange to see fellas hug? She didn't go in for the hugging in a big way. It was a bit of a palaver. They grabbed the bus to Rathmines and Jimmy talked about this lad and that lad and how he knew him from college.

*

The following morning she was up and ready to go home, offered no explanation to Jimmy for the sudden visit, but when he accompanied her to the bus station, he took care to wait and see she made it onto the bus, bought her a Double Decker chocolate bar and a copy of *Woman's Weekly* for the journey. And he waved, he waved her all the way out of the bus station and then ran through the doors out the far side, weaving among the smokers and their luggage, to wave her from the other side as the bus turned on Gardener Street, the Loopline Bridge behind it. She could still see him waving as the windows swallowed up The Customs House and the bump over the Liffey. All was not well and he knew it.

*

The bus took a detour down Burgh Quay, was this a detour, or was this the route? She couldn't recall the route. When they passed O'Connell Bridge she peered out the left side to see is there any hint of where Bewley's once stood with it's milky coffee-eyed students remembering how she didn't like the smell of the place, the stink of dropped milk, like there were crevices they could never scrub it out of. She marvelled at the memory of the girls in their get-up, all black and white aproned and Spanish as soon as they spoke with their *th* lispy English, all that coffee and ordinary women like her in for the tea, yes tea. She considered tea. She left him only four bags all the while knowing he'd need six. Would he have rummaged to find where she'd hidden the box? Would he have driven to the garage (shop) and if he did, which brand would he have bought? Lyons, green or gold blend or Barry's, would he have seen the box, does he even know the tea they drink? The nip of anxiety hastened and she worried about the post. The postman would have knocked the kitchen window as he passed, giving her the time she needed to put the tea towel down and go out to the back door and grab the letters from him. Would the postman have knocked the window, found her not there and stuck them under the plant pot? Would they be dripping wet? What if it was the television license demand? Her husband insists he will not pay for the telly license, but unbeknownst they have one. And if the renewal came these two days would he enrage and rip it up? And what of the kettle? Would he have boiled the bloody thing dry? And those carrots wrapped in plastic in the drawer of the fridge, she must remember them today or they'd begin to sweat. Maybe already on the turn? What of the gap in the back door? Would he remember to stick her balled up sock solution into it to prevent the mice from coming in or would the house be hopping with mice when she walked back into it? He wouldn't have turned off the immersion and it would have run all night. At least she'd have hot water for a bath when she stepped in.

*

When it's back she is, her husband has little to say. He speaks in factual clips.

I came down to see whether you'd be on the early bus and you are.

A kind of what about that for a revelation, as he opened the boot of the car. Of the magazine in her hand,

Give it here to me I'll put it in the boot.

—I'll hold onto it sure, she, clinging to it.

The nose of the car traces out the bend of the road and gives way, as and when another approaches. You're so squeezed in these parts, she thinks, there's no sharing the road, you've to roll into the ditch or slide past sheet metal. A neighbour, Matty, chooses the slide, he pulls up and ceases, the window down before he stops.

—How're ya getting on?

Her husband must lean and call to Matty even though he's right beside him.

—Where are ya coming from? Matty wants to know. But he doesn't wait for the answer before another *ceist* lands.

—Did ya hear poor Dick Gaughan was taken in the night, says Matty.

—I did not, Her husband. Sure I was down to see was she on the bus and she was. I didn't hear the notices, hadn't I the house left before they came on. What happened him?

—I don't know, I don't know at all, Matty repeating only that it was on the death notices this morning, I am on my way to get the story beyond.

Almost as an excuse for having nothing to add to the news of poor Dick's demise, or his having missed the notices this morning on account of her not being present to turn on the radio for him (she's certain he omitted to turn it on) her husband shouts over again that he hasn't heard.

I hadn't heard I had not, he repeats. Sure she was up in Dublin, I'm only after fetching her off the bus, up visiting Jimmy she was. I didn't know would she be on the early bus, I only went down on the chance to see was she and she was.

And she's livid. She's livid with no explanation the way she has lived with no explanation. But today will be saved by talk of a funeral, talk of a funeral provides for them all.

*

Jimmy phoned, he phoned while his father was out in the fields.

—No, no I don't want to speak to him. How are you?

He inquired again and again. Grand, she said, I'm grand. I had a good time with you and we must do it more often. I'd love a picnic in the Botanic Gardens, just the two of us. But he doesn't extend another invitation. Instead he asked again whether all is well? I'd love to see those pink signs again, she replied. What were the words? Repeat them to me. The one above City Hall. And the other on the bar.

—There was none on the bar mam, Jimmy said softly.

—God bless now, she told Jimmy as she closed the line. She promised to write him a letter tomorrow. He loves letters does Jimmy. I'm seeing them pink words everywhere, she sighed to him. She saw one on the bar alright, no matter that Jimmy didn't see it, he only had eyes for his lads. She searched for the words. *He'll never find another the like of me to put up with all his nonsense*, wasn't that it?

EPISODE 6

She regards her husband carefully. His face? Droopy. There's no other word for it. It's unkind, but the man is droopy. Two long lines surround his mouth, give up to jowls that jostle when he shakes his head. His eyebrows remain above his eyes, but are nothing remarkable. His ears are the only aspect of him unchanged. His forehead and flimsy hair have held up well, but when she takes it all in she cannot fathom how or why another woman would let him near her. There's so little to recommend him. And yet a woman has taken him and he has taken this woman and there's nothing for it, she must investigate the very bones of this transaction. She must undress this mystery vest to its threads. She can stand here in this kitchen and continue to know nothing, or she can head off out into the world and figure this muck out.

*

I would have to go out and figure this muck out.

*

At the time I began looking and carefully looking: Himself slid to sitting. In his sitting he was constantly looking. And where I was once looking only at him, now I was looking at everything but: I was looking out from him.

*

I, still furious, took a while to notice that he was now seated.

As I had stood up, he, strangely, had sat down, sat right down and stared.

And I hadn't done anything yet.

*

Still he caught my eye.

The first morning he stared into the middle distance like he was examining dust in the air, waiting on it to form an image, a message, an answer.

*

Slowly he emitted. Dribbles at first. After Tuesday's auction in Ballina: a man by name, the price not got, on the cow so deserved, the sinking of them all. Everything handed across to the fate of another's cow that didn't sell at a fair price because at that time there wasn't a fair price to be got. We're being skinned, he said. Farmers are being skinned alive.

*

I, remaining furious, paid little heed. I'd paid so much heed, now I was on strike.

*

See how I went back and forth?

*

I found him sat in the chair in the middle of the night once.

I went to bed with him still sat in the chair and woke to find him still there in the chair.

I was glad not to share the bed with him. I stretched out and enjoyed myself. But I worried when I saw him in the chair, relentlessly in the chair.

*

He started not changing his jumper. Socks stayed on him several days. I could hardly bend down at his feet and remove them. I could have I suppose, but I chose not to. Have her remove them I thought. Had he removed them in the bed of Red the Twit? Let her take them off him.

I did give in.

I gave in because the smell off him would knock a pig.

—Give me those socks you have on ya, I said. He obliged, robotically stretching out his foot so I might retrieve them. And when I saw the state of the feet on him. Painful and neglected they were.

He was, I must say, obedient in this state and that was not inconvenient. I still hadn't done anything.

*

Soon however it became difficult to watch him sat there and so wasn't I forced to leave the house. We had swapped: him inside, me having the car, off to Ballina to pick up feed at the Co-op, for the cattle would die for the lack of food and care.

When I was out and about I began to see an odd cut of the world I'd never noticed. Like Himself advised I would go in and sit places and sometimes have a bowl of soup or a cup of tea for my trouble. Once I even had a piece of pie in the morning.

And since he wasn't rising from the chair I opened the back door and started to attend to things. It wasn't pleasant nor unpleasant. It was a chore. Another chore. Chore after chore. The neighbours asked after him. And I told them a sort of truth.

—Sure he's killt with all the work, I said.

Oh it's a killer, they all agreed.

—It'd drive you to despair, I said.

It would, they agreed.

I was glad to get out and about a bit in it. For too long I had been inside.

*

It was more difficult when day after day he sat in the chair. Speechless, he sat. Read the paper without remarking much. Unusual, disturbing. While he was ranting Our Woman worried less. Now she worried hard. She had no idea what to do with him. She thought the cattle prices had him in the chair and sure there was nothing she could do about the cattle prices.

She sent two cows to the factory without his permission. She got a man to bring them in for her and he docked her money. You don't get a fair price these days, he said, handing her a pittance. When Our Woman told Himself she'd sent the cows to the factory she hoped it might spur him up from the chair. She hoped it'd make him cross.

—Very good, he said, you did well. How much did you get? You did well, he repeated, without listening for the answer.

She elected not to explain that she had to send them because the bills were piling. Nor did she say she'd no idea how long he might sit in the chair and she couldn't rely that he might feed them into the winter.

She paid the bills that time. Everything except the phone bill. She left that one to mount.

If he wasn't going to do his chores, they still had to be done. Our Woman had to get out and do them.

Briefly she decided how much feed to buy and whether to treat for fluke.

And then one day he stood up again and announced he was going to look for a trailer. All would be well if he found a trailer his arm gesture said.

*

I had been looking for the muck when I was out and about.
I'd paid attention and d'ya know it was going to be a great deal
harder than Red the Twit suggested these things were. I had no
man express any interest in me, other than throw me the odd
sentence at the Co-op between the aisles about the weather
or a bit of chatter down the field that usually was only asking
after Himself. I'd swear every one of them was in a coma.

I still could not fathom how he'd done what she proposed
he had. I was perplexed agin. Furious and perplexed. But the
bigger fear was at me: would he sit down again? While he was
up it was great but if he sat down we'd be sunk. I could not
allow for it and a plan formed in my head. A plan that had
to be got on with. A hunt.

*

In a place with a window that looked out on the street, the
hunt commenced so if what Our Woman must watch is too
unpalatable, she can avert her gaze. She began in the place
where all of it commenced, that bar of the hotel where Red
the Twit originally found her. The place she sat down for
soup. She began where he told her to begin. In the window.
Everything is in the window.

Beside her a conversation unrolled about what happened
behind a nightclub last night. It was unpalatable, so she looked
out the window. If she was forever looking out the window,
how would her hunt begin?

*

It took a further six weeks and three bowls of soup over a few
visits to the same place, just as she'd concluded it untenable,
then she spied one, ginger-haired male, humpy towards mid
forty, who it transpired came through the hotel near weekly.
A greeting card sales-man, fat-fingered, with wide thumbnails
she noted each time she saw him drinking a cup of tea.

It wouldn't be long now, for what would a blabbing fella like that do here, in this place, at night, only be hanging about, so certainly, when she went into town, whether it was for animal feed or the library, she carefully positioned herself in that place with a cup of tea, late afternoons, every week, and tracked his movements.

Lonely and predictable he was, having no one to care of in the town, except the shopkeepers he visited every few weeks to hawk his cards at, and talk his do you know any Haggerty's in Cobh conversations – so her presence eventually led to nods and greeting. Being a salesman, he was swiftly stirred to sell her something. Velvet cards, he tossed. Had she heard of such a thing?

She listened with is that right? curiosity in her face, solemnly infused with language of feigned interest (perky question) and deep attention (would you ever, I never knew that now, very interesting). She used the good eyes God gave her to stare at him. This fella needed attention the way birds need nests, so he'd pick and pluck and lift and twist whatever he could grab. He couldn't grab much blather from Our Woman as she's unusually careful in what she'll reveal in this instance, having in her mind a much greater purpose for him that required little in the way of discussion and more in the way of disrobing. Her strategy was to keep him on this path. When he talked of the velvet cards he could order for her, his tale of how he'd the official business and the sideline and he was talking to her now about his sideline she told him warmly hadn't he great initiative, while noticing the collar of his shirt very mucky on the inside by his neck where he sweated. No woman to mind his collar or no woman properly attending to them. He was a sweaty man, but he'd do. She contemplated her strategy of what she needed to do with this moist, nervy salesman, while he persisted with the line his cards could change the lives of many around her. She half listened, and mentally bumped

brain to limbs and decided today, yes today would be the day
to move toward him and collect whatever she needed. She
had to be clear and strategic about what she was looking to
understand. She hesitated. Could she stomach licking such
a dense specimen, as the licking according to Red the Twit's
description would be required? However, more heartily came
the thought, surely he'd do, because she was looking for a
quick insight, not a thesis on the matter. Thus she swallowed
and tolerated him through three pints – two bought with her
husband's money – an extraordinary length to endure such a
dull man. Giggled at his jokes, smiled at remarks and diverted
inquiries about her people and yes, that'd be great altogether
when he suggested he'd go upstairs to fetch the half dozen
mauve cards he intended to sell for the outrageous price of
three Euro. She prided herself on telling him he could have
the whole three Euro and not at all she would never take a
discount. And no, there was no need to bring them down,
she'd go up to collect them.

This was her move, all hers. Now she owned it.

His eyes noted this sprightly gesture. Awkwardly noted it,
mouth slackened a bit, brain too, surprise no doubt. He lost
his balance when he pushed back the chair as she watched
him calculate her intended boldness and blurted out how was
she for Mass Cards, he'd lovely harvest sympathy ones, apples
and a cart, pack of six, he could do her a deal a bunch for
twenty Euros. Wait now 'til we see, he said.

Upstairs, offered he did, a cup of tea, from his travel kettle.
*I've only the one cup, but I'll give ye a bag of your own – otherwise we'd
have to share,* him chuckling at his own gargle. Her, in order to
prevent him launching into yet another chapter of his life story
and who did she and didn't she know from bally-below, moved
and sat on the soft single bed, noting the dustbin, beside the
tacky side table had been decorated with a glued piece of white
lace. On the opposite wall, there hung a picture of the Pope,

arms out, his thumb extended. For some inexplicable reason he reminded her of a stout-legged rugby player, egging her on, saying come on now and don't be letting your team (the lads) down. Don't be weak, said his upturned palms, it may not be palatable, but what do you think your husband has been at? He was hardly trimming that woman's toenails now was he?

Card Man meandered on and on with snippets and jingles from life on the road until the kettle needed tipping and he paused to unplug and lift it. I'm very tired, she said in the middle of an anecdote about how badly repaired the roads were at some obscure roundabout in Cork, but if you've something specific in mind you'd like to ask me, please do, for I have a feeling I know what it is. But no, the silly man hopped backwards and threw his hands up at her in all politeness. *No, nothing, not at all. Except did she take sugar?*

She counted thirty seconds of his faffing and then undid her neat cardigan in a practical and deliberate manner, opened her blouse, removed it and laid it out, so it would not sustain wrinkles. Only her thermal vest remained, but since he was clearly thick, she left nowt to suggestion raised it over her head and tossed it on the floor in a move redolent of saucy ballroom dancing. An obvious flounce. She lay back on the bed and said nothing further. She considered that she must look very funny to him, a middle-aged woman in her tan tights and her triangular skirt, and her top-half naked, except for her Dunnes Store bra and the holy medal hanging round her neck. He hopped and tripped his way over to her: smothering her with the nonsense she was a lovely woman, wasn't she, instead of remaining, rightly silent. He commented on the remaining bits of clothes on her, that's a good quality skirt, rather than the body she'd unwrapped. He then remarked, somewhat absently, he'd been thinking of going on a day trip to Wales. Had she ever been to Wales?

No she had not been to Wales.

She longed for the silly fella to shut up and the only thing that would shut him up was to put an obstacle near his mouth, so she stuck her hand up in a gesture to cover it, but like much of their conversation, he missed the plot, offering his hand to help rise her up. When she did not lift up, he rolled over her, nearly flattened her before apologizing and finally, praise God, put his hand on her belly.

The skin along her thighs virtually peeled in the clumsy struggle to unroll her tights. Once or twice she actively winced, but he appeared a bit deaf and simply added even more pressured determination to the task.

Ought she to somehow involve herself? Yet her mind was concerned with the inappropriate angle of him for the task she needed to attempt. She should have obtained specific location of the postage stamp lick as described by Red the Twit, so she'd have some kind of ordnance to work from.

She certainly understood her husband. If this encounter was anything to go by – at least this man had the manners to share his kettle – the encounter with the Red-Nailed Twit must have been unpleasant indeed, for she was not about to believe that women were any smoother at this business than the butter-fingered poking happening below her navel.

She watched the radiator on the wall, as he tottered about, still muttering how beautiful she was for her age, which emerged stilted in his language, a monotonous drone *had anyone ever told her she was a fine-looking woman*. It made her think of a crumpet, a stale one left in the packet and removed, inspected and remarked upon for having survived with no mould. She allowed the thought to pass, only to hear him yet again inquire *whether it was OK, like ya know?* And he wished to inform her lest there be any misunderstanding that he was not a married man.

She could not understand these men at all. Her husband could not be trotting out these kinds of apologies, so she found it flabbergasting to imagine him making conversation, until she concluded that like her in these situations her husband said very, very little. They were entirely alike. Together in this situation they said nothing. Apart they said nothing.

He, the Card Man, was not what the teenagers would call a ride. Frumpish and struggled with his belt, it was nearly sad to be troubling him. It would have been more appropriate to play cards with him, since he was clearly in need of an explanation, and had twice asked when did her husband die?

—He didn't, she replied. She restrained from adding she didn't have one, they'd sold out of them at the shops. I'd be much obliged to you, was all she offered.

Instead of obliging, he retreated into marital counselling. *Marriage is full of ups and downs,* he said, still struggling with his belt. *I'd advise you t' go to Accord, it's a great service through the church.* Belt off. *Very understanding people, so it is.* A wiggle, trousers lowering. *I'd go meself if I had those kinda problems. I'm not a married man. Yet. Hah.* He huffed and puffed on top of her and said you're great, great, you're a great girl the same affectionate way farmers talk to their cows – go on there and hup hup hup ya, hup there – and eventually as he moved about inside her, there was something heavy, flat and wedged about him. She tried to replace the two of them with her husband and the Red woman. It was not an enticing picture, for she could imagine the pallid state of her husband's engorged stomach flopping about unsavourily against the younger woman's tighter skin, yet she could also smell the reek of cigarettes off the woman, and knew her husband wouldn't like that. Nothing worse than the sight of a woman and a cigarette he'd say. In a minute and a half, she gained some understanding as to what may have driven him to it: different people inside different places at different times. That was all it was. She had had a different man inside her at a different place and different time and now she was going home to put the potatoes on and think about it as they boiled.

*

As the potatoes hopped in the pan, she thought about it. Small spuds that day, she'd reached the end of the bag. She still had a sticky patch on her stomach from the afternoon's antics that she intended to scrub off, but watching the spuds boil she thought better of it. She would observe her husband come in from the fields and see whether he registered anything different about her despite the only evidence being hid beneath a tired-looking jumper. It was the kind of thing after this many years of marriage that a couple should be able to track. If he figured it out, I will believe in God, she vowed. She definitely washed her hands. Five times. On the fourth time, she noticed the bathroom window was cracked. There was new information to tell her husband and she was very glad of it.

*

There was a brief lapse in time between them when she settled into bed that night beside Himself. He stared at the ceiling as though his eyes are searching for a new planet to rest on, betraying an allergy to the current one.

—I'll be late tomorrow, he said blankly, I'm going to Swinford to look at a trailer, don't wait on the dinner for me.

—Will you be back before dark so?

—I don't think so.

He had to have been back at Red. There it was. He was up her alright.

She turned off the lamp and the electric blanket beneath them.

He had noticed nothing because he was back up Red.

EPISODE 7

Himself started in on Jimmy. Small digs. Bigger digs.

—How much was it costing to have that fella at college? And if he was to be calling down so often wouldn't it be cheaper have him here at home, and put him to work about the place?

It was an awful peculiar stance he adopted with the lad already two years into his course.

—Wouldn't it be better to have him useful about here? Wouldn't it be better if he earned his own way to an education?

*

Himself sat in the chair by the fire. Increasingly.

Nightly he read the paper, remarked abstractedly that nothing was worth anything. Everything pointed to the fact that every young fella and girl had a degree and at one time it was worth something, but these days . . . Silence. You can see by it, when a man can't get a fair price for his cattle, you know something has gone off. It's not gone away off in isolation. Everything, everything is lost once a fella cannot sell his cow for a fair price.

An unconscious look about him, like he was in another place, shouting back in the distance after cars that had run over him.

*

Whatever was the cause of it, his father disliked Jimmy in a way he had not objected to him before. He was ungraceful in his attack. Our Woman can see that he has moved in on Jimmy because Jimmy did the very thing she made him promise he wouldn't do.

In turn she was no longer going to keep a cow for Jimmy. She dismissed the idea.

I was shocked. Shocked for his father's sake. I liked the fella. And then I didn't like him. I want you to get a look at him. He was stringy-looking. Tall, with a mop of curly hair. He was a quiet man. It wasn't that I expected he'd bring a man waving pompoms. But this fella was way too up in his head and it was not what Joanie said about the gays. See, he asked very few questions, so he did. I wished he'd asked more. We couldn't be sure at first why Jimmy brought him to us. That night my husband spoke to me in bed which was rare, usually he either reached for me or he didn't. As he'd say himself, I don't get into bed to get into a heated debate if I want that I'll turn on the radio where's there's plenty people with nothing to do but talk all day.

—Well, Himself said. There's something fishy about that fella. He's awful quiet.

—Aye. I never usually said aye. We were both beside ourselves. He's a quiet man.

—Why has he brought him here?

—Perhaps he thinks he's a nice man. A nice man for us to meet. We don't meet so many men.

—I don't like it, I don't like it at all. I want him gone and I want no fuss made. You've to get rid of him.

For a man who wanted no fuss, he'd a strange way of going about it. At the breakfast table he stopped talking. To him the

stringy one, and to all of us and when he left to go out down
the field Jimmy raised his hands, palms up, at me inquiringly.

—I don't think he's well. It was a pure lie, but the only way
to get rid of the two men was to invoke a set of circumstances
where no person would stay. He might have cancer. Maybe it
is that he's the cancer, I said. I had the idea to say it because
in the church listings at the back of the newsletter prayers
were offered for a man out Balla way who'd the cancer of the
prostate. It might be in his prostate, I said. We don't know yet.

The two of them looked mighty uncomfortable.

I'd mulled the whole thing over I was not telling a lie after-
all I had no exact science on what was happening in this man
or any man's prostate and it could have been full of mercury
for all I knew.

Has he been to the doctor? That was Jimmy. Immediately
skeptical, immediately practical Jimmy.

—I don't know, I said. Sure he never tells me anything.

And good and timely the stringy but quiet, watery man
said we'll go. We don't want to be a burden at a time like this.

I coulda nearly thrown me arms around him.

—If you could get the two o'clock train it might be as well.
I said it politely, trying to hide my pleasure, but basically I
wanted the whole thing sewn up before my husband came
back for his lunch. I wanted them gone. I didn't want to sit
through another lunch. Sure you'll be down again soon once
this is all past. I said it the way mammies say such things. The
verbal sweep of the hand, gentle feather duster smack to the
back of the head.

Jimmy knew it was all a lie. I could tell by him. He went
for the two o-clock train but he didn't go easy.

*

Slipped into the bathroom, slipped him into the bathroom,
the two of them, to get back at me, and if you could see the

size of it, small enough to topple over with one man in it, never mind two. Two! And, the Lord save us, how I paced up and down the kitchen worrying if someone would come to the door, come in for tea and need to use the toilet and how would I explain the sight of the two of them coming out and the what on earth question in their eyes of "who is yer man with Jimmy?"

Twice I went to the bathroom door and once I spoke.

—Are you in there Jimmy?

—I am.

—Will you be long?

—Why?

And I couldn't answer him. I couldn't tell him the truth. For the love of God get that man and his watery smile and his leather jacket outta there or we'll never hear the end of it.

—I'm feeling a bit of an urgency. A bit of an urgency to go like ya know. I might have a spot of diarrhoea coming on.

It was ridiculous, but I had to get them out you understand? The other fella answered.

—We'll be about ten minutes, he shouted. And I found that awful bold of him. Sure in ten minutes if what I propose were actually true it'd be running down the hall. I was tempted to call into them don't mind me I'll just sit on a bucket, but I held back. They were going. That they would not come out of the bathroom was minor. I decided if anyone came to the back door before admitting them, I would say *just to let you know the toilet facilities are out of order.* I'd keep the door between the kitchen and the hall closed. I had my strategy.

Finally, when the bathroom door opened, I strode after them to the back bedroom and asked to speak to Jimmy. Alone. They were stood, the pair, with two towels – my towels, I wouldn't mind but I'd used the one around the other fella under my feet that morning and meant to hide it away on the rail – around their waists and the stringy fella had his arm on Jimmy's back and I almost expired at the sight of it.

—I need to talk to you Jimmy. I had to reclaim him from that hand.

—Can you wait 'til I get dressed?

—No I can't. He followed me into my bedroom in his towel frustrated. What is it? Why are you acting like this?

—Who is that man? Who is that man and why have you brought him here?

—He's my lover.

Lover, oh the choice of it, that word of all the words he could have chosen to use on me.

—Ssssh, I hissed as though the word alone would lift the roof of the place, would you sssh?

—You asked me. Jimmy, lifting his arms up, cranky.

—Why did you bring him Jimmy? Me, keeping my arms down, but raising my voice.

—He wanted to see where I grew up is all. If you have to know. Jimmy, snapping at me like a ten-year-old who'd lost his toy.

It all sounded ridiculous, so I quietened to have Jimmy retreat back to the room, a stream of water dropped down his back as he stomped away, and I heard the fella, whoever he was, muttering he'd go and Jimmy insisting not at all, if one goes we both go. And humphing out some slurry about his parents being backward and daft.

Backward! Daft! I'd a good mind to go in there and box him around the ears.

What was he expecting? An open-armed embrace? I didn't want Jimmy to go, I wanted his father to think I could solve the problem, but despite my persuasion he was stubborn and determined. I expected more from you, Jimmy said. His father he could understand, but you, I thought you got it.

I do, I wanted to tell him, I do, but what more understanding can I have, given I married the man. I married a man and if you marry one, this is what you do. You organize the things that disturb him. I wanted to tell him to be careful if he marries a man. There are things to worry about when you marry someone.

Instead I just said nothing except: he is a nice fella, but you have to give me a warning about these things. A second lie, I had my reasons. He is a dull fella Jimmy and you can do better I should have told him.

*

I still had to get the pair of them to the two o'clock train without causing a riot in my hallway. Himself had absented himself to Balla to look at a trailer or some warble. Maybe it was up the legs of Red the Twit he was gone looking. I had my project, I'd things to manage here, I'd to get these two flumps out of the house before the man came home and got all hairy over them.

Jimmy, the divil roast him, was determined not to make this easy on me. He'd come to make a point and he wasn't leaving 'til he'd stamped it on the inside of my wrist. I coulda told him then and there that I had seen him go places no young man should be going. I shoulda let rip at him, but I didn't.

*

I knew the two of them were testing me to see how would I manage them. They both stared me in the eyes when we were in the room together, tracking my response. They provocatively put their hands on each other to get a rise out of me.

I was so accustomed to wandering into Jimmy's room and never finding him there and doing a bit of dusting or looking through his things, for I am a fierce woman for a rummage in there, that I went for the door absentmindedly after lunch, and caught the naked foot. I should have called, alerted them with a *hello there, very sorry,* but didn't. As I realized my mistake, I halted, my foot slid slowly so as not to make any sound on the lino, my eyes garnered a thin telescopic advantage and in at the pair of them I stared. It was my Jimmy in there and it was my right and duty to look at him. They held each other, nothing hectic, affection it was, not strong lusty passion though and Jimmy doing the holding, I was happy about that. The other fella'd no shirt on him, and Jimmy lifted up on his arm, and leaned across and kissed the man's left nipple. He stretched so far and went for the left one. Why would he not go for the more natural angle, the right? I'll tell you why. I'll tell you why in a minute. OK I'll tell you why now. He wasn't the right man for Jimmy and Jimmy was letting him know and accidentally letting me know without knowing he was letting me know, if you know what I mean. He would have gone right, but his brain sent him left. I am superstitious about these things. I only ever sleep on the right side of the bed. I gave my husband everything on the left all over this house.

One thing impressed me about that watery fella was while Jimmy was at his nipple, the fella's hand lifted over my Jimmy and landed on his rump, pulling him into him. It told me he wanted Jimmy, he would include him in his life and as he continued tugging, eventually Jimmy lifted his head up to him and they kissed a long time. I counted to twenty-seven in my head, twenty-seven seconds of a kiss, don't ask me why I was stood there counting, then I withdrew. I sat on my closed lidded toilet, put my head into my hands and wondered whether Jimmy's life would be ruined, if he sunk it in with this man. I was reassured by that kiss. If a man could kiss you for twenty-seven seconds, it was unlikely he'd damage him, for I have never been kissed for twenty-seven seconds in one kiss like that and I lasted fifteen years of an engagement of letters and shuffling and the odd poke. Jimmy would go a long time on that kiss. As well for him it was.

After that visit, Jimmy sent an angry letter.

Only to me now. Nothing to his father. In the letter he told me I was a terrible parent. He did not say I was a terrible mother, only a terrible parent. It suggested plurality that I was only terrible when considered alongside my husband.

That evening I mentioned the contents of the letter to my husband.

—Would you be bothered if someone said you were a terrible parent?

—I would not. I would not at all, for I've given my children everything. He went on to say that it would bother him more if they had criticisms of how he was around the farm. With his family he was certain he had done his best. But he was not as interested in his children the way he was about the farm. Always something to do and always a need to experiment he'd remarked before turning off the light.

*

—If he's studying in Dublin, why's he here every weekend?

Because I never replied to the letter, Jimmy started coming home more often, which delighted me, but truly perplexed his father. I could see him ripening towards something unpleasant. If Jimmy was here, he was not.

Finally it wasn't long and he said that was it. We, for he included me, would provide no more money for Jimmy to study. He had written and posted him a letter.

*

Jimmy said nothing of his father's letter. I said nothing outright about the letter. I did say he wasn't to worry that I was hatching alternatives. He shook his head and said no, he'd have to do it alone, he'd have to do it his own way and he wouldn't take a penny of our money now. Jimmy stopped visiting the next months. He was busy he said making plans.

*

Come here to me would ya. He cut him off because of the cattle prices. He used the man visiting us, but the truth was he was sunk by the cattle prices. Once he wrote the letter, he sat more and more inside in the chair and ruminated on what had been lost. I had to wrestle the financial reins from him, he was sinking the lot of us. That was when I firmly sat on the horse plan. I'd heard the talk of it about how the EEC grant could be got off them.

EPISODE 8

—We need a horse, I said one night when Himself sat, like an odour, dour in the chair, staring into the fire. Everyone's keepin' a pony and a horse. We'll have a grant off them. A bit of feed down. There's nothin' to it. Little work in them, only trim their hair. I'm going to find out. Talk to people, see how we get the grant.

—Very good. Himself, resigned. It's up to you. He was heading out. This was unusual he hadn't been heading out at night so much. He'd sat in worrying of late. He'd sat in worrying me.

I don't think he heard me at all.

I don't think he heard me say we're getting a horse.

*

I could tell when he was worrying. He sat in the chair with a vacant look about him and his knees go slack when he thinks. Down the well thinkin' it was. No use to anyone thinkin'. I made myself busy when he got this way and hoped the phone would ring, so he'd look up and ask who was that? He worried me much more quiet than ranting, you'd never know what he was thinkin' when he was quiet.

Increasingly around that time he was more and more that
way. Gone quiet. Gone thinking. Gone Gone.

*

Joanie said men who went that way, thinkin', should be
careful. They often kill themselves she said. I would phone
her and say *oh God he's thinkin'.* Tell him not to go thinkin' that
way she urged me, tell him it's no good to anyone. I couldn't
tell her what I thought he was thinkin'. I couldn't tell her what
I was thinkin'. Well now Joanie I am thinkin' of plunging my
two hands into the same hot water. She would have had a
Mass said for me. Even now I couldn't say it to her.

*

Joanie said I wasn't to worry about Himself if he headed
out. If he sat in thinkin' then I was to worry. Then I was to
phone her. She'd call up and force him to have a conversation,
that 'ud lift him outta the chair.

*

Bina said whatever happened I should trail him. Don't let
him outta your sight, she said. Whatever he's up to you've to
follow him and find out do ya hear? I told her about Red the
Twit. I told her what she said.
—Well now, she said, I never heard a stronger case for
following someone in me life. I'd nearly follow him for you.
—Or I could do likewise, I said, without suggesting what
likewise might be.
—You could, she said. You could indeed. I never heard
a better case for doing likewise in all my life. I'd nearly do
likewise meself.
—Have you ever done likewise? I asked her.
But she'd to up and go because she'd to get to Ballina and
she'd to call into the Co-op and she might even need the vet

to call out to that cow. That cow. *She's the eyes torn outta me head lookin' at her,* she said. *Only I've no one else to be lookin' at, I'd be demented.*

She left, pulling the coat around her, urging me that she'd never heard a better case of doing anything in her life.

I was not absolutely certain her anything was my anything.

But eventually later on when the time came and I told Bina what I'd done, she almost took a stroke.

Her anything was not my anything.

*

There came a moment when I gave up on my husband.

When I decided I was no longer married to him mentally and it was time to do my own thing.

I lost all hope when he told me he'd be home late and not to save any dinner for him. If I could no longer be certain he'd come in from the fields to my table, I had lost it all. There was nothing left for me to read.

*

Jimmy came home to us on a Sunday at seven o'clock in the evening. Out of nowhere he appeared at the gate in an estate car, with two short-haired young fellas, the boot filled to the hilt with boxes and belongings. The three carried Jimmy's life back into my kitchen in twenty-plus boxes as I stared on astonished, fussed and urged them to take tea and cake and dinner with us. They would hear nothing of it insisting they must return this night to Dublin. Jimmy entered his room and did not come out. He did not eat and gave us no explanation. I knocked and he allowed me leave him in a cup of tea, but nothing else.

When my husband came in from the fields, I indicated Jimmy's bedroom door.

—He's home, I said. But I don't think he fathomed the

information. He won't eat, I said. Again I can't say for certain that Himself heard me. Thus, the next morning, a tense breakfast awaited the three of us.

*

Stundered was my husband as the bedroom door drew in, and his adult son emerged in pajamas to demand breakfast.

—Is there tea in the pot mam? Jimmy airily.

I've never seen anything like the face on my husband, an awful sight, it was pain, that deep shock on his face like the years had wound irrevocably back on us.

Jimmy provocative: boldly announced his intention to unpack all his belongings and settle back in. Would I make porridge? A cheeky smile glinted from him in my direction. I looked at my plate mortified. What was Jimmy up to? He never ate porridge! He was dancing all over his father. God save me from the pair of them!

*

My husband took off to the fields, did not request his son join him, and left with a few options, I chose, in my foolproof predictability, to go in and help Jimmy unpack. He'd never find anything again if I didn't. I attacked his clothes, folded his underpants, socks and vests, neatly stowing them, and commenting on the matter of some being worn out. I was shocked by the variety of knickers he'd acquired while away at college. Some looked pricey. Why would he need such pricey knicks? I imagined my husband's face as he realizes he's toiling away with the herd in the field so his son could waste money on expensive, unnecessary underwear.

Alone with me, Jimmy was normal and cheery: I was delighted to have him home and snuck a few hugs from him. We exchanged a bit of gossip and speculated on the things he unpacked. He reflected on how and where he'd acquired some of the objects as he stowed them and whether he liked reading that particular book as he put it on the shelf. He assured me I'd love Thomas Hardy. By the time we were finished, his shelves were crowded. I wondered amid all this clutter how long he'd be staying? I didn't ask. We'll need to get you another shelf I offered instead as a hint. Honestly I hoped he was home forever, but if I said such a thing aloud Himself would take a broom to me.

*

—Is he still here? his father asked her the next day.
—Well of course he's still here, she said.
The day after he asked.
—And when is he going back?
—You'd have to ask him that, she said knowing full well his pride would not allow it. It might indicate he took an interest in such matters and he was keen to maintain he does not.

*

By all appearances, Jimmy was neither going back, nor venturing outside the back door. He merely lounged around the house. They slipped into a comfortable routine where she planned the day around feeding him and making him comfortable. They talked about painting his room. They talked and talked and talked and it was wonderful like the years she missed of her son's life were being replayed again for her. She was getting them all back. She concluded forcing him out of college wasn't such a bad move after all.

Every few days Jimmy asked her for money and she obliged him out of the housekeeping money her husband assigned her. She'd tell him the prices have gone up and see would he give her more.

*

It is a week before they officially realize Jimmy has moved home.

—So he's staying is he? her husband asked.

—I've no idea, she said.

—So he is staying then.

*

Several Fridays on.

—Is that fella still here? Her husband, asking – a mixture of bemused fear on his face and indignation in his voice.

—Last time I looked he was still here, her speaking flatly.

—What about it? Her husband, sounding defeated. If he's not gone by Monday, I'll put him to work. Her husband, in ideas, without taking his coat off. Between the fields and the front room. Back out the door.

Good luck, she thought, good luck in putting him to work.

*

On the Monday morning, in Himself stormed, lifted Jimmy's quilt, ordered him out of bed and into a pair of wellies and out the door to help with the farming.

—Fuck off! said Jimmy.

There was a lot of roaring, she put two tea towels either side of her ears to block the shouts of them.

The *you can't lie in your bed while we're all out working, you fucking pulled me out of college, if you don't want me in bed, you shouldn't a done it.*

Jimmy said fuck a lot, she noticed. He musta learnt it in Dublin.

Then she heard her husband hurl that *he is a waster, an idler.*

It was enough, in she swept and ordered him to the kitchen.

—Would you not carry on so? You sound like a lunatic, a raging maniac. Sure he's doing no one any harm.

—He's fucking doing me harm is the harm he's doing. Was gone, her husband, his words muddling before him, after him and around him.

Jimmy shouted that his father is a fucking wanker. Loudly.

—Stop would ya, Our Woman said.

*

And he does stop.
Immediately he stops.
Exactly how she raised him.
She's proud.
She's pleased.
That's her boy.
Home again.

*

Her phrase *not doing anyone any harm* bothered her. She thinks of Patsy's son.

Jimmy, still in his pyjamas, thanks her without thanking her with the following exclamation as he lifted the teapot.

—He's a lunatic these days isn't he?

Her reply, crisp and cutting: I don't want to hear of you near Patsy's son. Do you hear me now? He's only a young fella. D'ya hear?

—Don't believe young makes him innocent, Jimmy says it matter of fact. I won't go near him, but I can't stop him coming to me. And he'll come, surely he will.

—Well then that's different, she says, but I don't want you near him, if you follow me.

—I do, he says. I was never interested in him, he wouldn't leave me alone, he was always following me about.

She smiles at her son, believing his every word. Sure who wouldn't follow him about. But she has a headache thinking of the reason why he has come home and how long is he staying and how will she keep the two of them from killing each other?

—Be careful what you wish for, she'll tell her husband a few weeks later as she is pulling the switch on the lamp. Look at the mess you've put us in.

He's seething, he's silent. Jimmy has not moved an inch towards farming. Jimmy is in his room much of the day reading books or at the table taking tea or into Ballina with her on occasion. Her husband's strangely quiet. She has no idea what he's up to. But he's cat-like, an intention in mind that's impossible to read.

*

A constant boxing match between the two men evolves, that she's forced to divert and referee. She establishes an excellent system of feeding the pair. As one is in the other is out and she structures their lives so they won't meet each other more than twice a day. Her entire life revolves around keeping these two apart. Everything else has been suspended.

The girls in her gang are back visiting her again.

The girls are asking questions about Jimmy.

They want to know why he's come back.

*

Jimmy knew exactly when he was going.

He stayed with us for nine whole weeks and never made mention of an intention to leave. Over two months! You can imagine what this did to my husband. Jimmy came home to torture him, it was as simple as that. His parting gift. He came for revenge and he got it. And I can't say the man didn't get what was coming to him. I, unfortunately, only got what was coming to me once he was gone. I hadn't fathomed what I deserved 'til it descended on me and I am getting every millimetre of it as I tell you this story.

I had two separate strategies for dealing with the two of them. Carefully I directed one away from the other, looping them past each other like a piece of wool on and off needles. I trained my eye close on any sign Jimmy was near Patsy's son. I even examined the back and front of his trousers for evidence. Once I sniffed his socks, and after thought it ridiculous. I trailed that young man everywhere. Where he went, I went. The girls in my gang were delighted to have him laughing among them for he was great company. Sometimes they asked him how long he was staying. That was what we all longed to know. Just a short while, I told them. He has plans. I prayed he'd go, that the questions might stop.

A few weeks after he came home I knew we had a problem, so I drove him to Ballina to the dole office. I had to get the car away from his father, and told him to go in and sign on, that he may as well have the few pound he was entitled to. If his father had known he would have been ripping. The collection of the dole each week provided me with another industrial challenge with the two of them. It had to be picked up on a Tuesday at Foxford Post Office, not the local one which had shut down to a few days a week despite the Conserve Our Rural Post Office Protest I went to. I was almost tempted to reignite a new protest to have the Post Office reopen again on a Tuesday so Jimmy could get his dole without all this inconvenience. Listen, I wanted to tell those poxy An Post'rs, do you've any idea the pressure you are putting me under closing on a Tuesday. I've two grown men to co-ordinate here. It's like trying to make sure a tank doesn't run over an insect.

There were impossible Tuesdays. I could not get Himself to surrender the car and we'd have to walk the four and a half miles back the road to the post office. It was a long walk when it was a windy rainy day, I tell ya, the two of us calling conversation above the bluster, trying to make out the other's face, as the hair was blown from our heads. Now and again someone would stop and offer us a lift, but sure we couldn't risk it, word would travel . . . I gave her and the young fella a lift into Foxford . . . and word would get back to him.

Not at all we'd laugh to the driver. *We're out for a walk, this is our exercise of the day.* And they'd pass on and we'd stare lovingly at the departing back of the car and long to run and hop up on the bumper like sprightly eight-year-olds.

If I knew then what I know now I would have enjoyed those walks and discussions. I would have poured all my questions into them, I would have cleared up every small aspect of my son that was a mystery. Even the elements he might not surrender.

*

Other days, to temper Himself, I would accompany my husband to the cattle auction. I think he liked company in the car and the way I was willing to disappear into Ballina to do the shopping, have my bowl of soup in the window of the place he'd urged me to frequent and the very window where Red the Twit had spotted and sought me out, while he would mingle with the men buying and selling their bullocks and heifers and what have you, even though he only came away with more depressing news about the prices.

All the way home I would see the effect the prices were having on him and I mustered a great deal of sympathy towards my husband because it was certainly wearing him down and the situation with Jimmy and all its silence drained him too, yet he was clever my husband, knew better than to trouble me with it.

See, I had had to leave the kitchen table now. The kitchen table was no longer the place where my assumptions could be made and weighed. I had to be out in the world with my husband in order to read him and know about him. Our whole world was suffering from daily interruptions that were very hard when I look back on it, they were awful hard. They finished off the lot of us.

*

Grief wants to know if I ever knew why Jimmy came home the way he did.

—Honestly I do not. I have no absolutes. I can only tell you what I suspect.

—Yes what is that?

—I suspect he came home because he was furious with his small bit of money being stopped. But that wasn't all of it. I think mebbe he came home because he knew he was never coming back.

—On account of him joining the army?

—I think it has little to do with the army and more to do with America. Maybe when he went there he knew he might never return.

—There's lots of young people come back these days though.

—There is. But you don't know my son. Look at the way he left sure!

—How did he leave remind me?

*

He upped and left like that with little warning. Came in the night before and asked could he pack a clean towel from the bathroom for the flight?

—What flight? says I.

—I am going to America tomorrow, he says, I've signed up for the army, I've been accepted and will go to a military training camp before they ship me out someplace.

I had to sit down.

—Come again I said.

He repeated what he'd said.

—How will you manage your lunch? I asked him. I'll have to make you sandwiches for the plane.

He smiled at me I always remember that smile. I wanted to whack him with a hard stick and tell him straight. For the love of God stop springing these things on me. Mainly I wondered what a military camp was, I hadn't a clue.

*

One of the main ways I kept the two of them apart those last few weeks was to take Jimmy out on walks when I knew his father would be about the house mooching and so on. We had lovely walks the two of us. We'd comment on how much mist or snow was on Nephin. We'd look at the clouds and laugh that rain was on the way when it was actually falling on our heads. We'd joke about the drought in these parts. I took advantage of our solitude to instruct him. I had to instruct him on fellas. I was worried he'd ruin himself. Be careful if you choose a fella, I told him. Try to chose someone who won't go stale easy. Men are very difficult as they age.

He nodded at me as if we had an understanding.

*

On one of the walks he asked me what I regretted about my life.

—Very little. I said. Very little. I have had a reasonable life. I knew where the next meal was coming from and I'm grateful for that. There are some things I would like to understand but fear I will never get to the bottom of them. I believe your father may have been carrying on with another for a while.

—Impossible, Jimmy said. No woman would have him.

—You'd be surprised it seems. He pressed and pleaded for every detail and I spared him few.

She had approached me, some kind of evangelical outpouring to do with God but basically she told me he had put his hands on her and she'd come to confess.

—I don't believe it.

Jimmy was disappointed I had not sought to verify her story.

—Go back and ask her how he met her? And then confront him with it.

—He's an old man sure what would be the point. You should know.

Jimmy announced again it was impossible and that perhaps the woman had lost her mind.

—Men always think women have lost their minds I told him, I'd be very careful assuming that.

—You should not assume what she says is true because . . .

—Because what?

—Because no woman would go near him. I promise you that.

—I went near him.

—You didn't know any different.

*

After that conversation on that walk the two men ceased exchanging any words. Jimmy acted as if his father did not live there anymore and his father simply moved outta the way as soon as Jimmy entered. It was over for the two of them ever sitting at the table together. It was over for the three of us in fact.

*

The day Jimmy shipped out, I am ashamed to say with so little notice, he caught Bus Éireann from in front of the Post Office to Ballina and would change to catch another to Limerick for Shannon. I wasn't happy about it, as I was driving him to the bus I plagued him with questions.

—What are you going to do?

—Will you have a gun?

—What if you die?

—Then I'll be dead.

—It's too fast, I told him, it's too fast for us to be used to such information.

—Us? He snorted.

*

—I only came home while I was waiting on my papers, he admitted.

—I wished you'd told me.

—What difference would it have made?

I handed him a milky way, a can of Fanta and the paper. God bless, I said.

And my son was gone. Swallowed into the dirty windows of Bus Éireann. Not a great departure. Not the departure he deserved.

*

I returned to an empty house. My husband so accustomed to dodging Jimmy, up and gone about his day.

*

He'd be home one more time, he said. One more time before they shipped him out.

EPISODE 9

Discretion. Our Woman settles on a slow cooker of mutiny.

All everything she plots while making jam and cleaning cupboards. In every sweep of crumbs to the floor, she feels herself nearer to victory. A pony, a Connemara, the future, all in a pony. She continues to chime on about the pony to Himself. Her husband looks blank but curious. Who is it she's talking to about this horse stuff?

—Ah people who know about these things.

—Right. He says.

Whenever he says right he's never listening. That's a fact.

*

She enjoys that he cannot imagine she can conceive of such an idea alone. Since Red the Twit there's nothing she cannot conceive of. But he's right! There must be a voice of authority! She couldn't carry out or command such wisdom alone! And she has the precise pairing in this operation, for there is the overdue matter of her odyssey, once firm, recently derailed by the return home of the bickering boy and daddy. Finally she's back, she's up, she's flying, well more a bit of a canter, but he must rely on her for information. Act like she knows what he does not. She's watched men do this. Pretend they've knowledge they've no more a whiff of and then hold forth as if they have, while everybody believes them. Bang the hammer and everyone will hear the sound.

Himself is a man who cannot resist prolonging a plan, because it delays a decision and affords rumination and speculation. And lately his life has been spent speculating on the cattle in that chair and her providing the cup of tea to assist him. Even in cutting off Jimmy, he did it slowly, working up to it like withdrawing blood, took his time, slowly pulling the plunger out, 'til bam, needle out, cheque stopped. Nothing to swab the sting. She's diverted what she can to Jimmy. Few chunks from the ESB bill, but it'll never cover what he needs. And even then he sent it back by return post. I have it sorted mam is all he'll say. I don't need it. I don't need your pity is what he's saying. Jimmy thought she should have overthrown his father. That's a fact.

And now with Jimmy gone, plucked from her by a bunch of men in green with their tongues out hungry for his blood – she was looking for someone to blame and her gaze settled itself back on Himself.

*

The public library is the place Our Woman goes to find out about acquiring a horse, for it's full of information and people looking for a chat. A picture of a toothless flour-handed man in Iran, whose name she cannot pronounce, a man she cannot say hello to, interests her instead more than the horses. Each and every time she comes to Ballina library, she visits this book as if next time she opens it the man in the picture will talk to her.

Not much to boast of this library, but like the train comfortable as long as you get a seat. Four hours can pass in the company of a sniffing farmer or a factory worker, in on her tea break, to borrow the novels everyone wants to read.

Except Our Woman. Plagued with query she is, yet when she sinks herself into the chair, her anxiety settles until she departs. It's regretful she ever has to leave the library at all, many's the day she'd like to stay put and be allowed to mould away to her own finality.

Officially she's here on the strict business of horse-related procurement and pony knowledge, but drifts to books on Middle Eastern architecture instead. Her brain snuggling them intention-less. Nestling for a place to rest. Other library patrons wonder about her chosen books too. Since this is rural Mayo, people huff-to-ya, puff to-ya and comment: that a good buk is it? Usually they announce on the weather. It's gone very cold they might say, like this has happened in the past ten minutes unbeknownst to you. Sometimes they extend a quip about what you're holding. Very often they complain about the state of the country. These are the welcome interruptions of rural life. You wouldn't want people to leave you alone entirely else you might forget you are alive. Some days it could pass over you entirely. A woman, the cousin of a woman she hasn't seen for a long time, asks after her: you often meet people you haven't seen for a long time at the library, like they're hiding away in here from you. And the enquiry about what she's reading or the coughing, the sniffing or throat clearing of someone beside her and the odd beam that escapes across the table of what they call in the news these days *foreign nationals*. Folk who have done her much less harm than her own husband has.

One of her fleeting Ballyhaunis Bacon moments has just scraped by her, when the pork of her husband's action clouts her forcefully out of nowhere and she finds brief comfort in the thought of him, entering the factory to have his flesh separated from his bones for betraying her the way he has. Stood in a queue is often when such thoughts slap her.

It sleets through her and is gone. They go these moments.

She reminds herself, she's up beside him now. Awakened and sat at a more accurate breakfast table tho' it's uncomfortable on her elbows and conscience.

*

Today, opposite her, as she admired the photographs in *The Land and People of Syria* in the Portrait of Nations series, (she'd already read Libya and Nigeria) a young man, with dark skin, snatched a repeated gander over at the spine of her book. Our Woman obliged him, lifting it up on the table, so he can catch the title. Approach, she willed him, go on and approach.

—You're reading this book? Have you been in my country?

For a full hour, she had sat, desperate to go to the toilet, pondering that incontinence can visit women as they age with a sneeze and the state of Bina's kidneys, but not daring to lift from the seat lest he venture her way. There will be murder at the house, she'll never have the dinner made in time and Himself'll be in, hungry, looking for it.

She shook her head, no, no she hasn't. Closed the book, but hastily he dropped beside her, put his hand out to take it. Opened it to a map, his thumb – and she noted he has a perfect thumb, a young thumb with a clean nail, no nicks to his cuticle – pressed along a river as he recited guttery towns, until he finds the one he's after.

—This is where I was born, the young smile. He is handsome, his eyes are bright, he was not born here in Ballina that was all she cared about.

—Is that right? She could hear the language of inquiry return.

For someone to have been born inside the book she's reading, that's worthwhile. That these tiny mapped blotches have as much significance to Syria as Shraheen or Cloghans have to the entire island of Ireland. She'd looked at this book many times on the shelf, but never dared touch it.

There was something about the word Syria, always uttered in hostility and it has brought something decidedly softer along to her today.

She peered again at that depressed thumb, it's tiny pouch of browned flesh spread on that page, now she's interested.

*

She cannot believe this. She watched the clock, counted the minutes to see how long would he stay beside her. How long could she keep him from his actual life?

He was lost in his story as he traced it in the book. Though fascinated by the manner in which his hands navigate the page, she contemplated his face. He was youngish. She needed youth. Youth was her way to understanding. Unfamiliar youth. It was kneeling right beside her. Patience, quiet now, she told herself, take care not to scare the living daylights of him, aging lady.

And on he talked.

Comfortable he talked.

He talked as if he'd needed a chat for an awful long time, the words queued up to discharge out of him. Stunned into silence by his company. Company that couldn't last.

Within two months I had moved to Al-Qunaitara. It's famous for its fruit trees. And he continues his thumb-tracing-trajectory. *In my ninth year my father had some problems. At eleven, my mother died. I was sent to live with my aunt in the North* and he found the spot, his voice ceased and somehow he became aware of the fluorescent lights and the cramp in his knee from kneeling and she noticed he was wearing a security guard uniform. Can he take the seat beside her? She flipped pages back.

—It's the people I like, she offered, I like imagining their lives. The weather looks hot. She lifted pages rapidly back to a green-shirted man near the front cover: what's this bread he's selling?

The book rotated diagonal, but his head shook. *I don't know. Some kind of . . . maybe the man is Assyrian.* She agreed he looks like an Assyrian, she'd have agreed he looked like a man in the Texaco ad if this fella'd stop here alongside her. *I think this bread is from the West,* he said. The equivalent of O'Hara's fruitcake or a scone, she thought. (Hannah, a woman in her gang, cleans their machinery in the local bakery each night 'til two o'clock in the morning.)

There was a lull between them now that demanded the question: why did you come to Ireland? Or what are you doing here? But she won't delve into that bucket and opted to let such wondering dissolve into the carpet, where she placed her gaze. They sat, examining pictures, silent, together.

Something in the carpeting of small-town libraries absorbed her questions and wondering. She can't deliver them. She caught his eye instead, said nothing, let him turn the page and they continued examining pictures, not speaking. He could be good, she thought. Very good. But how were they to get from bread and bakeries and Assyrians to the place Red the Twit and her husband dived.

Slowly, slowly, now or you'll frighten him.

*

—We hear an awful lot of auld rubbish about your country, she told him, but I've never believed a word of it. A lie, necessary, she'd rarely thought about his country, let peace be fostered here. And he relented, offered the beam she's hoped for, the grin that said welcome. Come on in. Enter, she thought. She was ready.

By the time he rose, he expressed a strong hope he'd see her again. I am often here, she said. Sure you know where to find me. It's light, polite and specific. Find me, it said.

*

That evening, she scrutinizes her husband.

Took a good long drink of him. She hasn't examined him closely for years, his familiar features have blended into each other so much that all he amounts to now are a few ambling limbs and a bobbing head. Tonight she observes him closely. She will understand how his skin ticks. And into which dark corners his brain extends. She considers their lovemaking. Every few months or maybe longer, a hand, his hand, comes across her chest to collect her and tweak her nipple, sharply like he's opening a valve. No longer than ten minutes start to finish. She's glad of it. She read in a magazine that once there's none of it at all, a marriage is utterly sunk. Their marriage is not sunk so. She has always considered it quality.

Too much participation from her unsettles Himself. Say she grabs for him, he'll readjust himself beyond her reach. It takes him a long time, half the minutes, to find his way in, there's a degree of squishing below, against her thigh, for which she cannot identify a purpose, but once in – and sometimes he misses – he mooches about for a bit and just as she's registered his arrival, it isn't long before he's gone. Slack, rolled off her. After he's very silent, like his vocal chords have been sawn in half. Either he's exhausted from it or this man, her husband, cannot have undertaken the acts this woman, Red, insists he did.

She tries to calculate how he'd sustain himself to perform the plethora of moves Red described and wonders would his back hold up? The maths does not tally. Yet, wait now, she recalls how surprising that her own triangular shape did not put the salesman off. The way she'd laid like the lid removed from the biscuit tin. How could that entice? They're like dogs these fellas, they'd take a sniff of any old passing rump. Literally stick their noses square into it, she thinks. Angry. Betrayed. Squashed. Determined.

She must succeed at what this woman claims her husband did.

*

Are these only hints of my depravity? She thought further on the Syrian, wondering what she could get away with, as she swept the fireplace of a morning. Would he even oblige me? She imagines he wouldn't talk rubbish like that blundering bog man. She cringes in memory of *you're great, you're great*. Syrian baker chatter would be better than have you been to Wales? Was it too audacious of her to consider such a young man might want to touch her, when all he'd wanted that day was to trace the valleys up and down a map. But what was he doing in that library on his lunch hour, why would he approach her, only that surrounded by a circle of hostility and suspicion, it's oxygen he's after.

He could be lonely, looking for someone to have a chat to.

And she'll be certain she's there when the urge may strike him.

It could fail, fail utterly. Then it will fail. It will fail spectacularly and she longs that her husband might catch her in the midst of this Catherine wheel of failure.

*

This is Ballina.

Our Woman is reporting to you from Ballina, where she is walking boldly into the PJ section of Penneys with one thing in mind. I want to find The Syrian, if he is to be found. I want to make it clear today I am officially looking for him. If I should die crossing the road, it should be known I was searching for him. I am deliberate in this action. I am not seeking revenge. I am absolute in what I seek. I seek The Syrian. I seek The Syrian for my own purposes. I seek The Syrian to give me an answer.

It could be said Our Woman is attempting an overthrow on cartography. I will place Ballina and Syria on the same map. I will unite us west of the Tigris. West of Roscommon. A road map. We'll come off a boreen onto a modern stretch of road and bump back onto the boreen at the end of it.

*

A random Wednesday, around noon, she returns to the library on the expectation that lunch breaks for security guards could extend all the way 'til two o'clock. She sits with a horse book, and scans it. Then worried he may not recognize her unless she's reading the Syria book. She places it on the table, but reads the horse book. Curiously today no one male or female approaches and it's a lonely two hours reading a book that doesn't interest her. It's raining, of course it's raining, and a steady gang of people enter the library to keep warm and shake off their drops. The woman at the desk smiles and leans over to take library cards and Our Woman wonders has this woman a happy life and wonders what's in her fridge and whether the woman is wearing tights. Does any woman still wear stockings these days or have we all gone the way of the gusset?

*

En route to the car, parked at Lidl and out of time, she had the brighter idea to walk through the shops with an eye on the rails and an eye for her man in a uniform. There's only a few places he can work, since there's but a few shops that would protect their giblets from thieving paws. That would be Dunnes, Penneys and Guineys.

*

He was not in Dunnes. No sign of anything in Guineys except GAA shirts and a banner advertising a raffle for the local boys' Gaelic team.

*

The nightwear section, between an unfortunate lemon yellow set of slinky shorts and shirt with fuzzy trim was where she discovered him. He was happy. His face animated in recognition, first words, *it's you*. They were barely into hello when his radio cackled.

—Come on, come on. He signalled she should walk with him across the shop, past men's tee-shirts, boys' shoes, baby blankets. He continued to talk into the radio and she kept pace, while people passed, grabbed a peek that wondered whether he was arresting her.

At the cash till, there was urgent discussion about whether a woman who left the changing room had or had not robbed a towel and a pack of six knickers. The knickers they're prepared to let go, since if she has them on her they can't be resold, but not the towel. The Syrian was trying to understand the colour of the towel but there was some misunderstanding in the pronunciation of the word peach. Petch he kept saying and peach the girl kept roaring at him. Peach, fucking peach, for Jesus sake.

He took off to confront the towel robber, who feigned confusion at the doorway and handed it over apologizing.

*

By the time Syria found her again, she was in the boys' clothing section, attempting to give the impression she might have a grandchild to shop for, admiring football kits and wellington boots with frogs' eyes on them.

—Sorry. He pressed his two hands together in apology.

—I thought I'd call in and say hello. She said brightly like it was entirely normal to track down security guards who don't tell you where they work. How are you keeping?

—Good, he says.

*

—Have you been back to the library? he asked.

The conversation continued about the library and was interrupted twice by the walkie-talkie. Overhead announcement. The emphasis on the first syllable of his name. Halll im.

—That's me, he pointed to the ceiling. That's me. I looked for you at the library, he adds. There's another book I want to show you.

She's in quick, swift as he begins to step away.

—You must call down to the house and visit. I'd like you to meet my husband.

—Yes, he nodded, I want to come.

Another overhead announcement, Halim to the front counter. He ducked a bit below the rail. Squatted to his knees, ripped a page from his notebook and wrote a mobile number on it. Send me a text. Don't exit by the front door, go out the side or they'll know I've been chatting. Chatting said chutting in his accent. All the way to the door she repeated chutting, chutting. I've been chutting.

*

As they separate, he waves firmly at her. He possesses a face that could age him anywhere from late twenties to forty-five. She hopes he's closer to forty-five. She considers that he's gracious, soft and enthusiastic and on her return to the car she considers that he will not suspect what she has in mind for him. The windscreen greets her with a parking ticket. Worth it. Worth every penny. Each digit in that man's mobile phone number has cost her husband several Euro.

*

It's loud on the street, his phone breaking up. Is there a bus? She'll come and grab him. I'll pick you up in Foxford off the bus if you can get down this way. Sunday, Sunday is when he'll come. Sunday, yes come Sunday. Her husband

is going to Tubbercurry on Sunday to look at yet another
trailer.

—I want to show you the horses, she says.

—You have horses?

—Not yet. Not yet. But soon we will have a horse. My
husband will be very interested to meet you, she assures him.

*

—How'd she get a ticket at Lidl? Himself perplexed.

Met a fella,

knows a lot about horses,

invited him Sunday, he'll come, see whether one might fit.

—I'm heading for Tubbercurry Sunday.

—I'll cancel him. I'll tell him come another day so. You
need to be here.

—Not at all. Have him come and look sure. I won't be
home 'til late on account of the drive.

On account of the drive. Indeed not.

*

His name is Halim and by the time he arrived he looked
entirely different without the insignia on his shoulders and a
walkie-talkie mounted to his ear. Younger unfortunately – for
she hoped civilian clothes and a bus journey might age him.
She wants youth, but youth is fearful in its stretch backwards.
He stood at the bus stop in Foxford, not uncomfortable, but
curious-looking, like he'd never quite fit.

*

—Do you like it here? Tea tray down. Handed him plate
of pie.

—I do.

—Are you sure?

—Irish people are very friendly, he said before a pause. But this is the first time I've visited someone apart from students in the college.

—How long have you been here?

—Two years. He bit the pie edge gently. Hesitant Halim, Our Woman thinks, while fussing over how he'd like his tea and do they drink tea in Syria? Lots of tea. Tea like this? Not quite like this, but tea. Every time she mentions his country, he lights up. Except she has to keep reminding herself the name of his country. A scrimper of a beard that cannot decide whether it should stay or go and a set of peaty brown eyes, overwhelmed by eyebrows. His eyes are brighter or bolder than those she is used to, so she cannot stare long at them because they stare back at her.

*

Is he cold?

No, he's not.

Is he sure? She can get him a blanket. She can add something to the fire.

—Have they fires in Syria?

Daft question. But since he loves to talk Syria he's off transported by heat, fires and weather. She's gone to get him a blanket. His plate moves to the side table. He reaches in his bag, he brought her something. A stack of books. One, she can keep, three she can borrow

Borrow, she likes borrow. Come again, it says.

—Here now, she hands him the blanket but moves instead to pat it around him, slips her hand beneath his legs in the process, along the side, moving to tuck him in firmly further up his thighs. He's alarmed, just mild though.

*

I must wonder while I extract myself why I have nothing but the desire to keep pressing my hands all along the sides of this stranger. I could carry on up his torso until I reached his ears!

Who is this woman? And where has she come up with such bold ideas on an average Sunday, an average Sunday where Mass and refilling the milk jug and sugar bowl, lest there be an avalanche of visitors were previously the order of her day.

*

That snicker of alarm on his face fades to a smile. Is that a knowing smile? Would she know a knowing smile. She couldn't give a snap of her fingers whether it's knowing or otherwise. She thinks of that cheeky twit swinging her leg over Himself and Our Woman left out in the cold, back here sweeping floors, lifting newspapers and making a bed for a man laid in another. Leave no misunderstanding to chance she thinks, and pats Halim firmly across his belly.

—Are you all full in there?

Her hand drops low enough to indent the top of his groin area. I am wondering what you've got in there, her eyes say.

*

She had risen this morning and baked. Strange choices that should have alarmed her husband, but he downed his egg put on his boots and hat and took off through the back door allowing the unusual whiff of apple tart to exit into the wind. There's a visitor coming today, but no reply, only he was *agin goin to Tubbercurry* to look *for The Box*. A box has become The Box. He has looked at fifteen different boxes in recent months.

Too big, too small, too chipped, wrong paint, wheel wear, rust inclined, not wide enough, too wide.

—I'd like you to meet him?

—Is it the horse fella?

Sort of True: She had met the Syrian when thinking about horses.

Not Ascertained: The Syrian knows something about horses.

Absolutely Untrue: The Syrian is a horse fella.

—Is he coming with his wife?

—He is.

—Bring him down to the field and let him see which way the grass is. He left it there at that single instruction.

She imagined showing Halim the grass and asking his opinion on whether it would suit a horse and that made her smile. This young fella, with a key to his locker, and a few textbooks from the RTC college.

—I'd like you to meet him, she repeated. This will ensure he'll never meet him. The *I'd like you to* sealing it.

*

She checked which way her husband went at the front window. Wrong way for Tubbercurry that much is certain. Right way for Ballina.

*

Plants a kiss in his groin between his hip and his pubic hair. Delicately. Lip meets skin then she realizes where her lips are – and what's she doing here? Presses it decisively and removes it slowly, from that few-fingered-sized-space of hair-free flesh.

Purposeful she is. They'd been thumbing through a book on some mythical valley and she'd begun to tire of it, and that image of Red and her bare behind propelled her into sudden action. The first stage a blur, somehow she ventured belt beneath, while he continued reading undeterred. Raised the book obligingly, while she parted his trousers to discover practical cotton underwear, disappointingly so identical to her husband's she could easily mix them up in the wash. He obliged, lowered trousers.

Orange light.

On and found flesh.

She won't look up. Places her two hands into his thighs and parts his legs, same way she'd divide bread dough. There isn't room for her two hands, so one above, one below, his testicles squashed saggy, his penis against her palm, she's got him now, visibly harder, a good sign surely. Encouraged, she places her lips on the top of it, sneaks some dry kisses along, waiting for a protest of some description, none, 'til arriving near the tip, she pauses allows her mouth to fill with saliva before taking the tip in her mouth (as she had read in the book on Jimmy's shelf). Above he whispers something in his language which she hopes is it's my lucky day rather than whose old mouth am I in? She isn't entirely sure what to do now it's inside her mouth, but as planned, copies exactly what she saw the young fella do with Jimmy. The angle is very awkward, but she won't give it up, she'll do battle. Direction confuses her and there's a bit of crashing. Up with her mouth, and down with her hand. Hand towards mouth and back. Repeatedly. It's a bit tight and her jaw nags. She's not sure how well it's going, but his hand has extended under to establish her breast. It strikes her she has no idea what her husband of so many years would taste like.

She remembered how the young fella speeded up on Jimmy, and how he worked with his entangled hands. She must shift her position, which she hasn't planned for and then there's the lack of access to do what the young fella did to the behind. She's minus the squeezing. On her knees, she's managing the front end OK, still not the most comfortable, she tries to shove her hands around the back of him, but he can't quite fathom what she's up to and sits firm. Out of space in this arrangement it's all getting too sweaty. Her mouth is really having a divil of a time figuring out the angle and what is required. It tastes alright considering, there's a nice smell of it, but it's ever so uncomfortable on her jaw and his knees are crunching into her ribs painfully. Fifteen more, she'll endure. She lifts her head to mutter something to this effect, when he blows wet, spreads all over her hand and further beyond onto the sleeve of her cardigan. Just like that. The smell takes over the immediate air like cleaning fluid. So fast. She's pleased. That's all there was to it. Dandy. That it ended will close any need for conversation as to why it started. She can tell you nothing about his body. Her concentration overloaded on execution. All of it took place under a psychological tarpaulin. As normal as lifting a jug or stoking the fire.

*

All cleaned and rearranged and back sat beside him without a word of explanation on either side, his hand took up her bait, drifted over to her back and moved about in subtle, small motions depressed her flesh gently like he was trying to figure out – post astonishment – what exactly she was made of. Found its way to the spare roll or two around her lower back and delighted in it, lifting it lightly and squashing it playfully. And they stayed that way for the shortest while, neither saying anything, but he's happyish. She can tell this without having to look closely at him. He took one of her hands in his two and kissed it. Such a gentlemanly gesture, in comparison to her who has been furrowing around in this young stranger's groin like a cleaning woman who'd lost her brush in a bucket of water. Ridiculous it might be, but this is what Himself wanted, and she shall want it too, she scolded herself to stem her greater inclination which was to wail in shame and beat her chest for atonement. It wasn't bad, she thought. I could get used to it.

*

Somehow she is not satisfied.

The arrangement of him sitting was all wrong. He should have been on his feet or back. The two positions she witnessed her son. All the details of what she imagined – never mind the outcome – were not satisfying. It must be in the execution that the triumph is felt. The triumph that sent her husband returning to Red the Twit. Somehow she wants what it is she has seen, exactly how she's seen it. A need to be under two fingernails at the same time.

*

—So . . .
she hears Halim say unhesitatingly,
—tell me all about the birth of your children?
But she chooses to let it pass.

*

In the car back, neither of them say as much as she hopes they will, but a few times he thanks her for the visit and says I had a good time, like he wasn't supposed to. She responds with random questions on whether he wears glasses and where does he buy his food?

—You'll come again, won't you, she asks him. His exams are looming. Does she have an email? No, no she doesn't. You could write me a letter, I am always behind that back door, she smiles.

The rain at the bus station makes it hard to make out the buses but she chitters out that if he misses the bus she'll be happy to drive him and sure, she could drive him anyway, but no he's keen not to inconvenience her.

When she pulls up the car, he turns and places his two arms around her and she notices as he pulls backwards that he fondles her breast lightly through her jacket, a polite departing afterthought that calms her. He bends down to his knees, puts his two hands on the seat and thanks her, before pulling his bag on his back and walking away. He does not look back at her. And this is good.

Our Woman finally understood why Jimmy took up with men this way. There was something nice about it, she decided. Even when it was raining.

*

She scrutinized her husband. Again.

Back from Tubbercurry with little to report: the trailer, unsurprisingly, no good, fellas should not advertise things dishonestly. Their described state reflected nothing of the truth he rumbled. How those words rag at her? What is to become of us she thinks wondering if the evidence of what she had done this afternoon might be written all over her?

She was surprised how easy it is to move into another part of her day after the explicit activities of the afternoon. She's between regret and resignation, a nowhere-in-particular spot.

She looked at her husband and had the strongest feeling he never put a finger on Red the Twit, despite what Red said, for how could he lay with such a good feeling at him, as the one at her, and betray nothing of it. He'd looked so thoroughly miserable all these months and if he was having this kind of fun, surely his demeanour would have improved.

To tempt him, she boldly asked.

—Two men, homosexuals, what is it they get up to together? How would they manage it?

He eyed her astonished.

—What else, he said. Sodomy. Sodomy is what they do. He was shook. She could tell. She shook him alright.

—Is that it? she said. Nothing else?

Light off.

*

Unwritten bedroom regulation.

—What are ya doin'?

—You're tickling me.

—Stop would ya.

—Where are you goin'?

But she kept going.

—Stop that now. Stop it.

—What are you at?

But she kept going.

By final ascension she calculated it was the only time she had successfully managed to shut her husband up.

Two in one day.

*

A new calculation has taken up residence in her right brain. How to divide her desire between what she wants to do with her husband and her new, more unusual desires of what she must do with Halim? Overwhelmed by the disparity, I am reckless, I am now reckless, she thinks.

She is no longer paying careful attention to cleaning the cups and has noticed the tea stains remain on them after washing. The bathroom floor had begun to maintain its puddles. Specks of black gather around the taps. The towels folded with such regularity now take their time to arrive back on the shelf and stay dirty and slung on the towel rail.

One morning Himself shrieked: Which in this pile is the clean towel?

Unprecedented.

*

Only when a protest was erupting on the Six One news in front of me, did I allow myself to think about Halim. One of them Middle East places, you know all the red, green and white, the big banners and the bandanas tied around their heads that makes them all look like mad lost pirates. I was sitting on the sofa beside my husband when them scenes came on.

—Where's that, is that Syria? I sounded excited, but my husband did not notice and my husband, who's very good with the news, said don't be silly it's the West Bank, it's them bloody nutters again, blowing each other apart. And I waited a few minutes and sighed.

—Well whether they're nutters or not, I said, they're lovely-looking people. Look at the great faces on those young men, see the elasticity in their skin and the beards make them look wise when they're all but twenty.

Then I counted to seven to see did he take note of it. Had I heard the weather forecast today was his only reply.

I was transfixed. There was a fella, a bit of a look of Halim, his fist going up and down, more of a beard on him, and words just flying out of him and the translation was slow in catching up and back to Eileen Dunne. Her hair was so incredible straight and scientific in its exactness, after the surge of fists and arrhythmic flags.

—Wouldn't it be great to speak every language in the world like that man?

It was the daftest thing to say since the fella obviously couldn't speak every language.

—I like the way the women are all tucked in neat to their scarves. There'd be no wind at your ears.

Silence.

—I think they're great, them fellas.

—They're a bunch of bloody nutters and sure we've a country full of them now to go along with our own.

—I hope Jimmy gets one like him, I raised my voice a bit. One who'll be passionate for him. Someone who'd fight for him.

Then he'd a face like a thundery thunk on him alright. Oh Jesus. Up he jumped, changed the channel and didn't speak a word to me until the lottery numbers were drawn, when he observed aloud that the number seven was being drawn too frequently and there was something suspicious about it.

*

It was important to keep the girls in my gang calm. I was strategic. I phoned. I called in. I had to keep them all calm. I have a tactic for each of them. There was a remote chance they might call up and take a stroke at the sight of Halim straddling my chair. The way to keep them out of my kitchen was to be in theirs.

Once I was back in their armpits, they took a relaxation over me, I could see it. I could see by the way they sat, the way they told me the news of the day. Suddenly the demands were gone. They just wanted me here and here I am.

EPISODE 10

The doctor phones her early. Can she come down? He wants to check her blood sugar. It's most inconvenient for she wants to head to the Blue House first and begin.

Days after Halim graced her sofa Our Woman had a problem with her washing-up liquid. A cheap Lidl purchase made in Poland or Czechoslovakia – it won't clean the plates and dishes properly, no matter how much she uses. She paid attention to her breakfast chattels this morning, rubbing the outside rim of a cup forty-five times and imagining it as some part of Halim's body. The green scrubber attrition for such a thought she sandpapered her cuticles in accidental punishment. Everything that lay in her sink reminded her of her visit to the virtual stranger's body parts. Everywhere she placed her gaze, chunks and angles of his flesh seemed to blaze up at her. She still had her hands in the sink an hour later. Her cups were not traversing their way to the draining board instead they were rubbed, replaced and rewashed in the sink.

Our Woman's brain ached, as though fingers were separating it inside her head. A pain above her eye. Surely to God the washing up liquid could not induce such misery, it must be something more.

Should she be disturbed by her behaviour? Was this headache the manifestation of it? Had it caught up with her now, nipping her viciously and variously through her day to remind her of the plunge she'd taken into that man's groin? She wasn't sure. The revisiting of the plunge, yes, well that made her wince, but in truth, she was merely consumed plotting how soon she could repeat it all over again.

*

Is there anything as lovely as a nimble, young man the way that sweet Halim is nimble? I thought as I put the butter onto my husband's bread. He loves his butter thick. The pristine condition of Halim's skin, all flat and elastic and not swinging and flopping and clouting ya with the remnants of every pint he ever downed. God love them all for youth is far from wasted on the young, it is age that is wasted on the old. Give us some sweet suck at youth instead of all this wallowing and wounding. I'm sick with the wounding. For what have I done to have that twit deliver me such news? Fifteen years I waited on a sodden marriage proposal that was fifteen years coming. And these days I'd duck whatever is coming, for I am sure there's to be more. I have my hand out now for whatever might fit in it. There are times of the day I don't give a flat toot about what I am after doing. I think bally-ho and off I go and why not, but then I think of the face on the girls were I to tell them and how they'd suck air in so swift they'd fall over. Ah. I'll have a piece of fruitcake and think no more on it 'til this lunch is made. I must go to Ballina again and look for better washing-up liquid.

*

Halim visited again. No pie, no preparation. Just tea. Just could you help me with my English. That morning she read his essay, but was busy thinking of the parts of his body she had yet to see. The upper arm area between collarbone and triceps and inside his arm. The aforementioned left and right sides at his groin to higher up the sides of his stomach to his armpit. Areas that have become unappealing, drifted to paunchy droop, on her calloused, crocodilian husband.

The essay read. The tenses corrected. A few spellings changed.

—Tell me about your pregnancy. I want to hear everything, Halim said.

She offered a hot drop as distraction, which he accepted, but in doing so patted the sofa. Come sit. She asked him if he likes college?

—How many children have you? Halim, sitting, but not as close as she indicated.

—Three. All grown up. London, London, Dublin.

Does he want to see pictures, but he was not interested in pictures. He was not interested in their lives. He was singularly interested in how they arrived in the world.

—How long you married when you conceived the first one?

She thought about the question, considered correcting his grammar, and found it peculiar but was it any more peculiar than the aged helping themselves to his young flesh? Help The Aged she mused, Help The Aged Help Themselves to the Young. She can see the poster campaign. Watch her! Paws off! Stamped across it.

—I don't understand the question, she admitted.

*

Now she understood the question.

His trousers remain open and the back of her cardigan still rumpled where he lifted it. Slightly startled she lifted her head, pressed her hair behind her ears and both her hands return and resume sharing the book. She plunked half of it upon his left knee and the discussion about the book recommenced. His hand stayed at the back of her waist, as though it might respond again with sufficient invitation, she does not press her weight against it. But she did steal a glance at him, to see what, if anything had he made of what just took place, and he smiled at her, a knowing nuzzle of a smile that confirmed that whatever had taken place was damned alright by him. It was important in these situations not to say too much, she thought. There was a relaxation at her she hadn't known in a very, very long time.

—You have sexed with many men, he announced.

She shakes her head, her eyes say it all. Not at all.

—You have sexed with a man who has made you pregnant three times.

—Uh ha. Yes she has three children so if you wanted to see it that way you could.

—How did she know?

—How did she know what?

—That her husband would make her pregnant where another did not.

He infers she has had a long line of men. Glory be to God. But there is a man beside her on this couch with his trousers open, so how can she avoid this question?

—What precisely is it you want to know?

—I want you to sex with me and tell me if you can tell any difference?

—Grand, she says, but right now she has to get the dinner on and must put the potatoes on to boil.

*

She wants to consume, rather than be consumed. She wants to consume exactly as her husband has. She calculates there are two or three more things she must understand until she can release him from their arrangements. And in seeking to

understand them she had overlooked he may have his own
demands.

*

A drop to discontentment. Halim goes awful quiet on Our
Woman.

Fatigue at the prospect it might never be repeated, that she'll
not have her answer drills her into the ground, she caves in
at the kitchen table, spreads out her arms and folds her face
on them and allows herself to dissolve. The bump of her skin
against the dining wood, water from her eyes puddling where
it should have no permission, she gives everything up to that
wood. What if he will not come back?

All reason and common sense are being squeezed from her
forcefully like remnants of toothpaste out of the tube. I have
ventured into wasteland I'd rather not tread. I am broken,
she thinks.

*

Halim she hears nothing from. All dwindles to silence.
An inescapable silence for she's certain he'll send a signal. If
nothing else he's a man full of questions, and there's few in this
neck of the woods who'd answer them. She tries to imagine
Bina responding to his inquiries about childbirth, Bina'd
crack him about the kisser. These days Bina is besieged with
conspiring. She's a morning, noon and night conspirer and
she concludes every story with the words you see there might
be something going on we don't know about. There might be
something more going on, Our Woman thinks.

In her mind endless scenarios play out from Halim having
died under the wheels of a bus, despite the erratic nature of
local buses (two per day), to him raw with despair at what he
allowed her to do. What if he's devout? What if he's some
kind of devout she cannot spell? A kind of devout where the

punishments are high. Perhaps he's gone to his religious person overcome with gloom, wailing *she seemed like an ordinary housewife. I had no idea she was going to attack me and to be honest I felt sorry for her.*

*

—What's wrong?
—Can she help him?
—Of course she can.
A work locker. A lost key. Shirts in locker. Only one shirt. College this evening. He needs his single shirt washed and has no way to do it between work and school and he fears they are trying to sack him at work and can give them no excuse to aid them. They've talked to him about personal hygiene. They've complained about the state of his uniform. They won't let him cut the padlock off. No because they want to sack him.
—I'll come and collect it.
—Can you bring me a tee-shirt to wear?
She can. She'll see him in thirty minutes. What time does he start work in the morning? Nine, he pants.

*

He's waiting, agitated on the corner they agreed on, sits into the car, removing his jacket and unbuttoning his shirt. She pulls a shirt of her husband's from her string bag she uses to transport vegetables, brushing a piece of cabbage from the cotton.

He repeatedly thanks her as he does the transfer. He's awful worked up. Not at all, she says. Not at all, sure it's nothing. But he's stranded, how is he going to get it back? She'll bring it of course. The same spot. I'll bring it early she says because Himself will want the car. He leans over on departure and pecks her cheek. It's a boyish quick peck.

*

Once washed the shirt must rotate. It hangs above the range until her husband comes in from the fields. She removes it to the airing cupboard when she hears his feet on the path. After the dinner is taken and he's gone within to the fire, she whips it back above the range and calculates she can risk it hanging there, deciding Himself will not notice. Beautifully oblivious after Prime Time, he exits again saying he's to go back the road amid grumbling about the state of the country and how Fianna Fail will drive us all into the ditch.

—Headfirst into the bloody ditch is where we are headed, he laments.

Is he taking the car?

He thinks he might.

He might call in on a neighbour.

Once the car is gone the shirt is safe. The shirt hangs and dries until Joanie calls in and her eyes immediately light on it. That's a lovely shirt, she says. Eyeing it. Joanie's seen it and she'll tell the girls and they'll all be lookin' for it when they visit.

*

He comes again, Halim does.

Asks strange questions.

Again, he only wants to know about childbirth. She gives him details of her children: names and ages, hoping he'll respond with a clue to his own age. But no, nothing, so then she talks about their different personalities, searching his face lightly to see is this the information he is after, but his eyes dart at her and away from her and he's not interested in their Leaving Cert results or their potential in the world of plumbing, or nursing, or Áine's banking exams. He turns his thumbs, forward then back, frustration, something in the conversation is frustrating him, and this is difficult, she wants him comfortable, he must be comfortable for the circumstances already shriek sufficient with discomfort. Her, the old pillow she is, and him, so taut and well sprung. Warmly she keeps her eye on his, while considering whether to touch his arm and when she does, lightly just the top on his wrist, he blurts it out like she's given him an electric shock . . . the birth, the birth, how was it?

She's stuck.

Our Woman is stuck.

Her hand is on his wrist and his question is odd. Will it be even odder if she pulls it off. It would so she leaves it, but it's no longer light, rather she's clutching his arm nervously, uncomfortably.

—How was it? he repeats.

—It was childbirth, she replies. Uncomfortable, unpleasant, bloody and . . . would he like more tea? She lifts her hand away to go for the teapot. He does not want tea. He's waiting on her, he wants to return to childbirth. It is pure madness, live and interactive on her sofa on a Sunday. And he takes her hand and puts it strangely on his belly, like there's a baby in there. It's uncanny. Perhaps he has children some other place. Perhaps he has children all over the place. Perhaps he wants to import them. Perhaps he wants her to help him import them. She only knows whatever he has and wherever it is, it is not her business. If it were to become her business, it may make it difficult for him to sit on her couch. A scenario that wouldn't please her. She doesn't wish for anything that would make him cease visiting. And this is the reason she attends to it.

With her hand on his stomach and longing to oblige his request – was it, after all, so unreasonable – a man who came from a uterus having questions about what came from hers since he hadn't one of his own?

Well, she says, what exactly is it you want to know, I am happy to tell you if it really does interest you this much.

All of it, he replies. All of it.

*

Our Woman thinks back and commences. They lie against her couch and she talks into the space between them and the fireplace. Neither looks at the other as she soliloquizes and the fire handily cracks a bit to cover up the odd word.

Remember, she begins, I have had three children and so each birth was different. For starters they were all born in a different season and we'd different problems around the farm as each arrived. I delivered every one of them alone in a room except for a doctor or nurse who called in occasionally to ask how was I getting on and then took over at the end. In those days your husband was not allowed in the room while you gave birth. When my son was born my husband did not know he'd arrived for two days because there were a lot of problems with a sick cow at the time and he was out day and night tending to it and I had gone to Castlebar and stayed there and word had been sent, but we'd no phone then and well you don't want to know this. The worst birth was the first, my eldest daughter, it was an indicator of what was to come for she's a difficult and obstinate girl and pardon my vulgarity, but she has a very big head. I was offered a handful of blue and pink pills, which at first I refused, then seeing how awkward this creature was I requested they hand them to me again. They didn't make a difference, but my waters, which had insisted on not breaking then dropped out of me and my distant memory of her birth is that my feet were as wet as a penguin's.

He laughs.

Great, he's still alive, she thinks.

—I can only say to you that it was an inhumane experience that I vowed so help me God I would never repeat as long as I was in the full control of my senses.

—You felt no joy? No elation? He asks. You had no moment of completeness?

—I was stitched from my arse to my elbow. I was tired, I was resentful and I wanted to cut my own hands off.

—And then?

—Then I had a cup of tea and six weeks later I felt better.

*

My second daughter flew out of me with so little warning she nearly landed head first in a bucket. That's all I can say about it. To this day I am still confused by everything she says and she speaks in a terrible hurry and gives you no real information about anything that has happened or is likely to happen to her. If, though, you were to ask me which daughter you should marry, I would say my son, but failing that this daughter, for the older one has a vicious streak I'd be keen you avoid.

My son, Jimmy, was the last one obviously and since I knew I would not be doing it again I minded it less. It was not an easy birth but the hospital was better and I'll tell you the truth a strange peace came over me where I could have surrendered and died. I couldn't explain it to you if I tried. But when I didn't die and found I had a baby I felt not joy but certainly more contentment than with the previous two. And he was a very easy baby.

But Halim's not satisfied with this, he wants to know about the birth. Does it hurt? And if so how? Explain this pain to him. Explain how the stomach contracts. And how the body pushes out the baby. And could she tell when she became pregnant? He's pressing her for minute details, and yet here they are the two of them sat so peaceful.

She walks to the back door and puts the bolt on it. She scans the windows and closes the curtains. She turns off the light and leaves on a small lamp.

The best way to explain it is if you try it yourself. Here up you go. Lift your hips.

—No, no, he resists, no, no. He starts giggling.

—Really it'll be easier than explaining it. I'll demonstrate it to you.

—Back you go, she pushes him playfully.

—Lift your backside, she sticks two cushions under him.

—Now she says politely . . . I'll need your leg. She elevates his left leg at the thigh and calf and pushes it up and gently back so his knee is heading towards his ear. He cranes his head up to see what she's doing.

—No, no lie back there now or you'll ruin it. Your trousers might be a bit tight but sure we'll give it a try. Right. She pushes his leg back to give him the idea. Then lifts his other leg up to the back of the couch.

—Leave your leg up there, she instructs.

Then resumes with the left leg pulsing it backwards until his tendons begin to protest. Once it is as far as it will go and the seams of his trousers look endangered, she says lift your head and breathe. Then with her spare hand she presses down on his belly gently. This is where your womb would be and then her hand skirts the air in a circle below at his groin, this, she indicates, is where you feel dreadful pressure like the most bulging constipation you could ever imagine, like your hips will blow off and a giant concrete ball replace them.

He erupts in laughter, leg collapsing from the top of the couch.

—Let me up, he squeals, please let me up. She retreats politely and the two of them laugh in a different way.

—You asked.

—I did.

—And so now you know.

He reaches across for her. You are funny. He kisses her cheek, it's thankful more than presumptive.

—You are funny, he repeats.

—Have you a child somewhere?

—No, he says, I haven't.

*

Sacred Heart he's still curious.

How long she was married before she became pregnant? Tell him did it happen the first month? How many times did she do it with her husband, before she became pregnant? Did her husband do it in a special way each time she found herself pregnant?

It is time to excuse herself to the toilet. On the seat she allowed the run of urine extra time to give her space to think. What might possess a man to be overflowing with such concerns. He must be looking desperately for a woman to reproduce with. Do they teach the menopause in Syria? There are a lot of rumours about that country.

*

When she returned he has an even stranger proposal for her.

—You have sexed with a man who gave you three children.

—I have?

—I want you to sex with me and tell me do you find any difference between him and me?

She is perplexed.

—What? What are you saying?

—There must be a difference between the man that gives children and the man that does not. I want you to try to tell me what it is. I must know. He unbuttons his shirt.

—But I wouldn't be qualified to tell you a thing like that, she's distracted by his lovely sleek arms. She cannot get away from his youth and when she sees a hint of it, she wants it. She calculates which is left and right, and before he can say another word, leans over the way she saw Jimmy lean over the watery fella, and plants a long kiss on his nipple, as though all that stands between a man who makes a baby and who doesn't is such a missed kiss. He murmurs something in his language and drops his hands around her back. He cannot do very much else, since she has the monopoly on his chest, so patiently he waits 'til she's lifted her head.

—A woman has never done that to me before, he says pleased. It's precisely the kind of compliment she's received about her baking. They are on the right track. Hurriedly she queues up all the images she caught of Jimmy and his men and tries to choose which one should be next. She has no desire to sleep with him in the traditional sense. She only wants to experience that which her son gave and received.

*

Halim had his own ideas and they're nice traditional, pleasant ones too, unwrapping the various layers of her clothing, discarding them like onion skins, he's particularly attentive to the inside and outside of her thighs, but she will not give herself up to be flattened and submissive underneath him, so allows a bit of time at that malarky before she moves to the main thrust of her plan. Let's go out to the barn, she suggests, rising. He's startled. Semi-naked and startled. Barn? Barn?

*

In the barn she's not sure this is such a grand idea because she's anxious vermin might scamper over her feet. It's dark, very dark, once the door is shut, stinky, and not even a shaft of light between the two of them, they can barely find each other. It's cold, she regrets not bringing a blanket and there are objects to negotiate that she's forgotten about, but she's a plan. She must know what her son experienced that day and here is the man to show her.

—Like this, she pushes on his shoulders, encouraging him down to her hips, and he commences precisely what she has come up here for. Biology somewhat absent from the original equation. She dragged his hands to the back of her, but he began to wobble on one knee.

Technically speaking, it did not work as well for her as it had for Jimmy that day. She'd never had a man's tongue, her husband's, between her legs that way and though she found plenty to recommend it, with the bale of straw scratching her backside and the tickling out front, it required an extreme balance and itching concentration act, with an increasing number of goose pimples on both their shivering flesh. She never stands still in a barn, she is in, out and about to the animals. She has a moving purpose entering the barn. Plus she's aware of the sounds outside and realizes this is an utterly lunatic arrangement. Is that a tractor passing along the road? A wheelbarrow coming up the path?

She'd inverted the positioning: she should have had him receive her sucking, since it was that sucking action that had bothered her the most. The hungry gobble of that young fella pulling at her son.

She'd ruined a recipe.

*

His awkward attempt within this arrangement to penetrate her failed. She'd resisted saying *it's all wrong, not this way,* and he complained of the uncomfortable prickle at the top of his thighs from the hay, which was lacerating her lower back. He suggested a return to the house to reunite with the comfort of a bed, but on exit Halim tripped on a spade and fell rather badly.

Back in the kitchen the bloody graze his elbow took on falling led to medical repair and since she did a good nursing act, which he lapped up, that led to the kettle rather than further flesh and they sat drinking tea together as though nothing had ever happened between them. In the harsh light of the bulb, she was terrified to touch him, for this table was where she sat with her husband, watched him sigh over the salt pot and where she recorded the deaths of soldiers and civilians. Another problem was whenever Halim sat down with no purpose, he began complaining vociferously about all aspects of his life.

The strangest things happened when men sat down around her.

*

That night she doesn't sleep well. All Halim's questions about childbirth confuse her as to their purpose. And she must stop this nonsense. When she looks in the bathroom mirror, she sees only how worn out her own face is, and how age has ravaged her and suddenly he looks tauter and younger and newer and polished, more elastic than he is. She doesn't smile when she thinks of him tonight. When she looks at her husband in bed, his nose just above the covers, she belongs here beside this relic, where they're drooping in unison.

*

By Sunday her mind is made up. She will not ask his age. She's more to do with him and she must get on with it, that's a fact.

*

As a matter of fact I must carry on.

*

Sunday and Halim's low. He's awful down.

—I can't stay in this country, it's too hard, they treat me very bad in my work. They think I am stupid but I am from a good family, I study hard and yet these people treat me stupid.

—Don't mind them, she tries to cheer him up, but he won't be cheered.

—My life is awful. I have disappointed my family. They had big hopes for me you know. I am from a very good family, he repeats.

—I'm sure you haven't disappointed them. And you're young, young and studying. I wish my son was still here studying.

He is briefly interested in her son, but wails further on his disappointment.

He repeats that he has disappointed them and he cannot tell her why.

—Nonsense, she says brightly. Go way outta that.

—You don't know anything. Nothing at all. You think I'm stupid. All these Irish are the same. They seem like they like you but actually they hate you. They think I'm not capable.

He's morose in this state, so she whisks herself away with the kettle's boiling.

On her return from the kitchen she brings a tray of tea.

—Sometime I will tell you about my wedding, he says.

Please God save me from it, Our Woman thinks. Offering him a Kimberly biscuit as consolation.

*

After that visit she settled on a pony, a Connemara pony. A lovely one with an overgrown fringe she could attend to and be shut of these morose, immodest men in her ears.

*

But first she'd another thing to do with him

EPISODE 11

—Are you still having the visions?

—I am.

—And how are you managing them?

—I am doing what you suggested. My kitchen floor is ever so clean.

We laughed. It is important to reassure Grief, to let her know that I am behaving in my widowhood.

Everything else we discussed faded into the nice room, the nice floral lamp, and the cosy beige chairs we sat on. We could have been exchanging bingo numbers. All I knew was I was sat here for my reputation and for the Blue House. The Blue House with the gaping big hole in it.

—Kathleen, she told me warmly at the end of that session, you are doing very well. Much better than before.

I was not talking about the naked men. I was behaving. Progress had been made. For some reason I was Kathleen instead of Phil. I think she had confused me with someone who was doing better than I am. When I phoned to book my next appointment I called myself Kathleen. Whoever she was, she was doing better than me.

*

People assume a mother to be protective over who marries her daughter, not me, any man who wanted them could have either of mine, if he'd a clean face and a warm hand. I never worried about my girls. Especially the eldest, I knew she'd be grand. I raised them that way. I raised them strong and indifferent and they knew they'd only have my attention when they practiced it and neither of them let me down.

*

When the girls were sick they'd push me away and take to the pillow, not Jimmy, he'd cling to me like a clawing rabbit, he'd sit on me, hang off me, drop around my ankles if I stopped still. I could see him physically hurt if I had to go out to the kitchen to turn on the kettle. I never slept a night that boy had any illness. I sat in the bed, hand on his piping hot head, I talked him through the chicken pox, the measles, there wasn't a thought or fear that child didn't share with me.

*

Jimmy's the only person in my life who ever gave me a fright. No one could give me a fright the way Jimmy could. I had a terrible pain worrying about Jimmy serving himself up to the wrong man, yawning his way to the beyond.

*

—I have days where I can't remember whether I have buried my son or not.

Am I forgetting things? Grief asks, perky today because I talked first.

—Yes. I am.

Can I remember that I buried my husband? Grief asks.

—My husband is always dead, I never forget the day I buried him but I am very confused about Jimmy.

Grief wants the full extent of the confusion.

I'm too exhausted to explain it.

Take your time. She sits back, waits. Would that she were just a little more impatient.

*

Everything about widowhood is exhausting because you're trying to recall, unable to recall and then expected to explain why you cannot recall. It is not as simple as living. It is not as simple as being irritated. Being alive and married is like sanding a windowsill. Maybe it is dusty, it may get in your eyes or knick your fingers but you can look at it and see there's a windowsill. You can look at your husband and feel no need to say anything to him.

The curse of the widow is the non-stop chatter outside and around your head. Like a television talk show where you loathe the questions, but cannot turn it off. Miriam, Miriam, Miriam go away with your nice gentle questions.

*

I walked to find some peace.

They thought I was walking for madness.

I was walking from madness.

*

It was true I gave them a shock. I concede this much to Grief.

—You gave them a shock, Grief informs me at my weekly appointment. If you are going to give them a shock then they're going to be afraid for you.

Was there any need to be afraid for me, she wants to know. Was I a danger to myself?

To be on the safe side she is going to have someone from the Health Board look in on me.

EPISODE 12

Bina worries they'll send me to Ballinasloe. She tells me so. If they ship you to Ballinasloe you won't come back.

If they take you, she says, you need a witness here to record it. I won't leave your side.

She's good that way Bina.

*

His father took a few days to notice.

—Is that fella gone? He asked indignant.

—He is.

—Well glory be to God, I thought he'd never go.

I lay down in our bed and cried quietly for as I already told you I do not like to invite questions when I cry.

His father had not asked where his son was gone.

*

—Is he coming back? Himself requested when eventually I rejoined him in the kitchen.

—He has gone to America to join the military. He only came home because he was waiting on his papers.

—And how is it I wasn't told?

—You weren't in the night he told me, and you were up and gone the morning he left.

—He never should have come home at all.

Words. Rolling pin to pastry.

—He only came home because you forced him outta college.

—I did nothing of the sort.

Stubborn. A considered pause.

—Isn't it as well for him. He's too soft. And soft as he is, it was you made him that way.

A pause. I choose not to fill.

—Now come again, where is it he's gone and what has he joined? It could be the making of him!

I could not tell whether I was sad because what Himself said was the truth, or whether I was sad because for all his ferocity Himself genuinely seemed taken with the idea of Jimmy in uniform. I could not say it was no good thing, for I would risk usurping that brief moment of approval.

Instead I told myself that his father, above all of us, was the most ambitious for Jimmy. Himself believed Jimmy'd thrive with discipline. He was right that Jimmy would not thrive the way I had made him, if I could only tell you what that referred to.

*

The only thing Joanie says she heard about anybody making anybody anything around the homosexuals like ya know is a programme she saw on psychology where she said they said that a baby born with his nose up to the heavens rather than down to the floor may have a predilection to being a gay.

I stare at her.

—And what do you think?

—I'll tell you the truth it is the biggest load of auld rubbish I ever heard. How on earth would which way your nose pointed affect it? It'd be more likely to make you allergic to pollen.

Then we go back to discussing the benefits of Manuka honey which Joanie says is mighty for every single thing, there isn't a thing it won't cure, but the price of it would lift the skin off the roof of your mouth. She pulls a tiny jar from the cupboard and we put it in our palms and stare at it.

—Eleven Euro. She says.

—Eleven Euro!

—Lift your tongue, she says and stuck a spoon of it into my mouth.

—There now, you'll sleep better with that.

*

I had three letters written and posted to Jimmy by the first Friday week. Just short notes. But I missed him, I missed him terrible. And I woke nights imagining him hurt and burning. Hurt and burning were always what I imagined.

My husband will tell you it wasn't long 'til I was taken strange. He'll tell you it was on account of the boy's absence I became strange. I'll tell you different. My gang will tell you different. There was nothing the matter with that woman is what they'll tell you.

With Jimmy gone and my husband absent so much, it was easy to bring Halim to the house. I contacted him regularly for the bit of distraction because I enjoyed him. I encouraged him to come down and visit. I offered to wash his shirts. He was a great man for needing shirts washed. I seemed to be washing shirts that weren't worn, but what about. I could tell you I initially contacted him for a bit of distraction from Jimmy's abrupt departure, but actually my mind was full of other thoughts. I was not finished with him.

*

Quickly Halim noticed how depressed I was and asked why I had been so quiet with him, was I angry with him?

—My son was home and is gone and I am missin' him
awful, I said.

—Yes, he said, I can see. You are very dark in the eyes. Your
husband is a bad man, no.

—No, my husband is an ordinary man, not bad, it is me
who is slowly demented. The cattle prices are causing pressure
on all the men around here. My husband more than most.
It's all he talks about.

*

I took Halim on walks with me.

We walked the routes I previously took with Jimmy. I said
he was a nephew from England. I thought about the things I
planned to do with him.

One neighbour said he looked like a Pakistani and was he
a Pakistani? I agreed he was. From England he is. A Pakistani
from England is he, the neighbour repeated. He's a very good
man, I said. Oh they are, the neighbour speaking. They only
marry their own. Were you ever in England? I wasn't, no I was
not, the neighbour said. I've a brother there but I never went
meself. He broadened into how you'd have no peace from the
cows if you took off too far beyond a day in Ballina. They're
always at you. Like children sucking at you. Chores to be done,
they always need something from you. Like children they are, he
repeated. No, I corrected him, children go away, cattle do not.
We slaughter them, remember. Maybe he'd better carry on, he
said. I believe it was that man who may have reported me strange
or strained to my husband. It doesn't do to correct a neighbour.

Another neighbour, again a man, for the women come
to the door to make their inquiries, or look at you queer an'
squint if you disturb them, passed us another time in his car.
He rolled down the window and asked pointedly about Jimmy.

—No that wasn't him I was walking with, no, no that's a
relative from England.

—I haven't seen your lad about, he continued. What took him?

—He joined the army, I said and the man's face was jubilant within that car window. *Isn't he great, won't he go far, he'll do well out of it. I tell ya, I tell ya, I tell ya. I was surprised to see him home and knew he couldn't be staying long and now I hear he's gone to the army, well it all makes sense!*

He drove off with an air about him like he was off to make a cake or build a good fire to celebrate my lost son finding his way.

*

That was the conversation that started the talk in the bank. The talk where they said Jimmy had gone because he wanted to get away from me. That he went to get away from me. They never mention his father only me. It is only me he went to get away from. Do you hear that? They are joyous he finally escaped me.

I walked home with a short stride and long heart, my tongue so heavy in my mouth I could barely keep from biting it between my teeth. Nobody knows my son. Nobody but me. He will not go far, he will not do well out of it. He'll come home in a box out of it.

*

That was the night I was taken strange, my husband later told them. He said I'd come in from outside that day with a *confused* – confused being the polite local term for possessed – air about me. She didn't look right was all he'd say when the doctors asked him. The Lord save us she was confused, others would say, which is the polite local way of saying she was raving out of her mind.

*

My husband had it all wrong.

The others have it all wrong.

I wasn't taken strange over Jimmy at all. It wasn't 'til weeks later that I was officially taken strange and it was on account of Halim, not Jimmy.

*

It might be true that the night before that Sunday Halim visited I was feeling a very small bit demented. I went through the catalogue of events, the things that bothered me so much about what my son did and the things I have seen. I revisited every one of them that morning but was struck with a curiosity that had never poked me before. The duplicate bodies didn't seem so savage and I wanted closer in on them, to examine them more carefully. I wanted to recall those arms and those legs and those lips on those nips. I became frustrated when I couldn't recall it precisely, for previous I never could shut it out of my mind. Now it was sliding from me. Jimmy's absence taking all of it, more than I wanted gone. No sooner is something gone than we must know more of it. Why's that? I often felt this same way when a cow leaves to the factory. I've no interest in the animal, but once missing, a hole forms for her. I look for her. I miss her in a whole new way.

*

Things were slipping from us: me and Halim. Whatever we came together to do had an inevitability and we shoulda just got on with it – left the talking, the walking, the thinking alone. Instead we slipped into too much chat and comfort and that was an awful bad idea. Things can get sloppy around the teapot. I see that was the trouble in it all. I confused the objective. I blame myself. Was he, in the end, too nice a man for what I had in mind for him? For Halim too was beginning to burden me.

*

During one visit where I ironed a pair of trousers for him, Halim asked again why was I so saddened. Where was my son?

—My son came home I said slowly, for a reason we didn't understand and now he is gone for another reason we don't understand.

—Leave him alone and he'll tell you eventually, Halim said.

I didn't like it.

I didn't like it one bit.

Here was another man presuming to know more about my son, than I, his mother, did.

I didn't like it at all.

I wouldn't stand for it. He was stamping on my patch in a way he wasn't welcome to tread.

*

Halim came to my kitchen again, but we had to reacquaint ourselves. I could hardly recall how forward I had been to him and that afternoon I commenced polite and distant. I made no move to hug him on arrival but there were sexual things I longed to do with him the moment he sat down. I've never been clearer in my life about what I wanted to do with someone. There were two items on my list, but I remained female and farmish, indecisive how I was to make the ascent. He did not seem disappointed. He had two shirts for me to iron.

—I see you found the locker key? I laughed. So much trouble at work, he said. One woman in particular was gunning for him.

—Why do women do this? he asked. I am from a good family and they treat me so bad there.

He watched me while I iron. He watched me closely. Every time I moved past him his eyes were on my hips. I wanted to put my hand under his chin and tip his eyes to my eyes. Up here Mister. But his gaze remains fixated on my pelvis.

It occurred to me this could be useful.

In turn I lowered my gaze to his pelvis. The back not the front, which meant a bit of craning my neck. I had begun to do some thinking.

*

He made only one gesture. As I am coming with the teapot, standing, he, sitting, grabs me about the waist and presses his cheek against my belly which I had already sucked in and hugs me strong wrapping his arms around me. He murmurs. I had the teapot uncomfortably above his head and my elbow was wobbling. I did not want to tell him to get off. One eye on the back door, I'm aware the things I want to do with him are not finished yet. He stayed like this long enough and strong enough to convince me this is the time to do them.

*

It may not have been the time.

*

If he hadn't made that stomach gesture I doubt I would have proceeded. But he dared me and I was invincible in this state with him. I wasn't in my ordinary life, I was in an extraordinary moment in my ordinary life. And he had presumed to know something of my son, which angered me, so much so that I must prove he knew nothing.

—Come, I told him, once the pot met the table. I want you to see my son's room. I watched the clock. I'd no idea when Himself might be back but I can't risk his catching me. We were safe until the hour of hunger.

And once in Jimmy's room, I closed the door pert and swift. Laid me down on Jimmy's bed positioning myself as the watery fella had, while Halim browsed items round the room. I reached my hand out and tugged him, he knelt beside the bed watching me. A pat of the mattress and up he hopped. I began to work on his nipple exactly the way Jimmy did with the watery fella and tried to remember what came next.

Before I could recall the sequence, his hand slid up my leg and seemed to be examining the shape of my pelvis rather than vagina. He darted around my vagina messing about with his hands like an engineer. Measured his hand span across and down.

—Will you let me do something? he asked. Tentative. I like tentative. Tentative means permission given is permission owed.

Whatever he was so polite to request permission for, I had bolder plans for him.

—Work away, I said.

*

The problem with Jimmy being gone was not just that he was gone, and gone off somewhere dangerous, it was we'd so little information about what he was doing.

Since men and women can faithfully never agree on what to worry about, I put this to my husband.

—Aren't you worried about him?

—Not at all, sure it's the first time that fella has been useful. I'm not a bit worried about him. I only worry about idlers, men who sit about thinking instead of getting on with it.

He admitted he was proud of him.

—I like the way he took us by surprise. I didn't think he had it in him. I might even write and tell him, Himself said.

*

I lay and thought and thought and lay and I could not see things the way my husband did and after this amount of marriage perhaps that should have surprised me, but it ceased

surprising me many years ago. I paid close attention to the
news and I began a system of recording the war casualties
on the bottom of my table mat. I had the notion that using
a process of subtraction I would be able tell if my son was
killed. As far as we knew Jimmy was in a training camp in
Pennsylvania or some place beginning with the name Camp.
I was anxiously waiting on a letter from him. I stopped
sleeping well at night, indeed I stopped sleeping at night. I
would wake with the fear at me, that Jimmy was hurt and
always so close to me physically, yet I couldn't grab him.
Men waving bayonets clustered themselves into my dreams
and all I could see was men with their hands around each
other's throats and in their last minute frightened, regretful
eyes that seemed to appeal with words like I'd rather be at
home mowing the grass, it wasn't what I expected and why
am I here anyhow? In my dreams Jimmy was always fighting
like World War I, muddy and in the trenches. Even though
he was in Pennsylvania and in one of his seldom letters had
described very modern equipment, bunk beds and plastic
cutlery.

*

Women in scarves with anxious eyes were looking at the
camera. But those women had their arms crossed or they raised
them up, like they were holding invisible hammers, in defiance.
They might be crouched or backed against the garden wall,
but I admired the way they kept their arms crossed. A kind
of you have me, only you don't have me. They reminded me
of Bina: sometimes what she's thinking is far more powerful
than what she might be saying until she delivers it up to you.
When I saw the soldiers rounding them up or putting them
down to their knees with their arms behind their heads I
couldn't see my Jimmy doing that. I couldn't see him binding
hands with plastic ties. I couldn't see him yelling get the fuck

down. I couldn't see him in any of it. I couldn't imagine how he'd keep the goggles on his eyes nor the pack on his back. And I worried the size of the boots they wore would give him blisters. I wanted him home, I wanted him home without the boots, I wanted him home this instant.

*

It's a very dusty place Iraq.

I bought the RTE Guide and carefully studied it for all or any television programme about anything to do with the Middle East or the army or soldiers. I ordered a satellite dish unbeknownst to Himself, who when he almost tripped over it coming in the back door barked in alarm what in the name of Jesus is that thing?

—It's a dish for the television.

—What? What would we need this for?

—We're going to have to be watching the news in Kuwait now Jimmy is gone in the army. I told him in such a manner that suggested if he didn't shut up I would bounce the bloody thing on his head.

—He's in Pennsylvania, he won't be going anywhere for months. He'll be home before he goes anyplace.

—I don't want to hear another word about it. You'll put it up on the side of the house tomorrow.

*

Grief seems upset with my question. Had I made my son into a homosexual? My husband says I turned Jimmy soft. Does soft mean homosexual? Is that what soft means?

Grief, in voluntary capacity, assures me this is likely not what my husband means, but since my husband is dead we have no way to verify.

—I did want him gone. Well I wanted it gone.

—You did?

—Yes.

—But I also wanted it to stay.

—How?

—Everything that I saw I've longed to see again and again.

—What do you mean by everything you saw?

—I saw Jimmy at fellas and fellas at Jimmy.

—How do you mean?

—At each other literally.

—In your house?

—Yes.

—That must have distressed you.

—I thought it did, but now I see that I loved to see it because it showed my son was alive and I want it all to come back. Because in wanting it all to be gone, it meant all of it and I wanted Jimmy gone, maybe more than my husband. And once he was gone I wanted him back, so very badly, certainly more than my husband.

—And now that the two of them are gone?

—Were you ever in the bus station in Athlone? There could be four buses parked and you're sure you know someone only you don't, but by the time you accept it, you climb back on the bus. I never get out of that bus station.

Grief did not push me. For I would have had to say I am only waiting to be gone myself now. Isn't that the final instalment, hanging around in people's way as they've to step around you and about you?

—I've a new friend, I told Grief instead.

—You do?

—Yes. He lives in Limerick.

—He, is it a man so?

—It is.

—Well, Grief said. That's wonderful. Except, she said, it was important to take things slow. And she said many women rush into relationships.

I had to shut her up.

—Oh no it's not a relationship, I said. He doesn't actually like me, I said.

—Wouldn't that be a bit tricky if he's to be your friend?

—Not at all. I said. As long as he doesn't throw something at me.

Grief returned to talking about my daughters.

—Now tell me the latest on your girls and the sleep situation.

Grief is so interested in my daughters, I almost expect her to proffer adoption papers.

*

—I want you to do something for me, Halim repeated. He'd asked twice, so he must have something filthy in mind. Perhaps he did know something of my son after all.

—Anything, I said like a horse with no harness.

—I have to know what the cervix feels like.

—Very good, I said, work away, thinking he meant sex.

*

It's not ideal, not precisely her plan, but there are worse things to do on a Sunday and there was a time wasn't there when she thought it would be a very good idea. The time when she determined it necessary to understand the beef of her husband's actions.

—I want you to know I have read a book on it. Halim reassuring.

—Grand, she says. Get on with it, she thinks.

Some budgy fingers 'til she realizes it's a physical examination he's after, like the doctor, not the usual manner of squish-against-the-thigh let-me-in entry.

—You mean?

—Yes.

—I don't know about that, she says.

—Please?

—Go on, but be careful. For God's sake be careful.

Whilst it's not the most appealing thing she has ever experienced, it's not objectionable enough to tell him to cease and she stacked up her generosity and once he retrieved his fingers, *he couldn't find it and the book is all wrong*, but he's glad he tried. He said it is interesting up there, the abstract way you'd talk about a strange coloured bird up a tree. Isn't the colour of its breast remarkable?

*

He'd one more request.

She was practical, pragmatic.

—What is it? She clucked before adding a curt, whatever it is would you just get on with it. Men such ditherers! She recognizes she'd be hard pressed to see her husband any more assertive in these circumstances.

Silent his hands meandered her mid-riff. Little interest in a traditional sexual act, she couldn't quite fathom him, he was ordinance survey mapping her reproductive functions. The palms of his hands and fingers splayed and stretched on her skin, his thumb and first fingers pointed, stretched one either side against her skin, to locate precisely what? She'd no idea. He rotated her legs down from the bed, they trailed the carpet, parted them as wide as they'd go and manipulated her groin with his forehead. It was mighty peculiar. She could not figure what he was up to, only felt some kind of gentle head-butting motion, as though he was trying to push his cranium back into her. She'd give him a maximum of two minutes at this lark before she'd lean to her final request, that she'd been deliberating on. She could hear his voice again those months back instructing her on how she's to be with her son, as though only he, in his boots, might understand him. Leave him be, she heard, he'll tell you when he's ready. We'll see, she thought, we'll see how much you understand him. We'll see now what you know.

Halim was smiling pleased, after her allowing the head in the groin rummage and she wondered for how many years of his life he wished to undertake this exploration. How many women had rejected such a request? How many women had he filled up trying to parse his way to the mystery of the cervix? She looked at him and realized he was a tender young man, who, for whatever reason, no matter how many women he might fill, would always have an empty hole. Never, he exclaimed hushed, did I think I'd get this chance and it's exactly how I imagined! Can you still have a baby? he asked absentmindedly.

*

Her request, in comparison, was tame. And he was awkwardly bemused by her instructions, squinting and staring down at the top of her head, his body a tad stiff and tickled by her nippling. Her insistence that she repeat the nipple sequence until it was perfect confused him, up on the elbow, she instructed him to act indifferent, then become aware and he wasn't entirely convinced by the requirement to fling his thigh over her, suggesting it'd be more natural if she flung hers over him. They rehearsed and rehearsed. Now we'll do it properly she said. One last time. He was generous and didn't question the what and why of this nipple fixation. It's like a play, Halim laughed. Exactly, she thought. Precisely.

She'd moved onto hand gestures to illustrate so there might be no misunderstanding: her final request. Her skirt she hitched and indicated her rump. To tell him this is where you are going next! She ensured her hand pinpoints his destination precise. Make no mistake about it she did not flap vaguely about the kidneys, but as she did so it dawned on her this might not replicate what she saw Jimmy do by that stone, since Jimmy was doing it. This wretched inversion time and time again. But it was too late. The request had been filed.

She pointed out the window.

—Out there!

There was a very interesting pause. It was one of the more interesting pauses of her life.

Halim's arms flew up. His head retracted slightly.

—Absolutely not!

He began to wave his hands like he was signalling traffic.

—I never do that. No way I go in there! On my mother's life!

She laughed, a hearty laugh into the calm that followed.

She offered tea. She was furious. Furious that her ascent was cut off, so near the top. In protest she did not scald the pot.

But she's vindicated. Ha! A wholesome vindication.

—These are the things my son likes to do. You don't know anything about my son, she said quietly.

She watched him to ensure he'd heard her, but he had not. He had not registered a word of it. He was still looking out the window.

She wanted to be both her son and the man who hupped him.

She didn't want what Red wanted.

*

At the table there was something slightly stunned about Halim. Like she offered something but with no place to put the image it stuck in his throat and rendered him speechless. They won't discuss it. Never, she thought. If he tries, I'll tell him to go. Not to worry, yet again he trod back to childbirth.

—Is it true that the leg ligaments stretch endlessly while the woman is giving birth and how do they go back? Halim wanted to know.

The Lord save us, the man's devotion was inexhaustible. She wondered would she have taken him up that field? She imagined her husband coming upon them. She could have defended herself. This was what I once had to witness. I had to find out how cold and uncomfortable it is. But she would have frightened him in a way no man deserved to be frightened. His wife would have been irretrievably mad, rather than momentarily mad.

*

She was not finished with Halim, if he won't go in there, she will.

EPISODE 13

—Can you remember when your children were small and the words they said? Our Woman asks Joanie recent.

—I don't know. Joanie, cautious. Do you want a hot drop?

The dodge to the teapot. They're all doing it now. Trying to keep her off the subject, any subject, danger, trouble subjects.

She'll not be budged.

—What's the earliest story you have?

—Oh I don't know. There are so many.

—Do ya know I've less and less. I am losing them all. She tells her by return post.

—Come on 'til we'll measure the front window for curtains. Come on now.

*

Years back, when her girls were yet young and Jimmy not even born – as life is now: girls not young and Jimmy gone – details nestled tight in mental crevices. She could confidently look and not lose the shape of things so quick.

Today, thinking, on the Blue House beside her, she has the shape of the old woman, who sat in front, screaming instructions at those within and changing her tone whenever anybody passed. She can hear her.

—How're ye gettin' on? She'd call out to not quite hear the reply. When you passed her she'd turn again.

—In the name of God how long am I to sit here shouting for a spoon: are you all dead in there or what? She'd curse them.

Today, the poor repair, the present state of disintegration is not obvious, she can only see where the blue of the windows once sat, but since peeled and flaked into overgrown grass, so paint nor house nor garden are indistinct from each other. A protruding tree from the half-collapsed chimney declares neglect like a flag. It is a house dismissed. Fit for nothing. There will never be a good fire inside the grate again. Demolition would be the pale ordinary man's verdict.

*

All incidental.

*

Still she does not have the story of its discovery. The when and why and how the Blue House invited her in. This is frustrating. She tries again. She must try harder. She must listen for it. Then maybe it will come again.

Was it Jimmy who remarked on the house, it must have been Jimmy, otherwise she would not have noticed it, but there's no retrieving what he said. All her Jimmy moments feel like they've rolled under a cupboard and she cannot quite reach them, even with the handle of the broom extended. Whenever she can't find a story she cries and she doesn't like this, she wants the story for herself, rather than the inconvenience of a wet face needing swift repair when knuckles knock against the window, the way the knuckles do knock, or a voice calls out, so regularly around here. *Hello within. God bless all here.* Hello. Come in. It can feel like there is a set of teeth in through the back door every hour. Rap tap tap tap. All the different knocks she has come to identify. She'd love to roll under a cupboard and just wrap herself around the molecules of the story she cannot quite trace.

*

—Mammy.
—Yes.
—Where are you?
—On the bus. Me, talking on the mobile phone that Áine, my daughter, insisted on buying me and insists I carry everywhere, even into the toilet. There's only three numbers in it.
—What are you doing on the bus? Áine, talking in my ear, via the phone she insists I carry.
—You're breaking up. I lied and pushed the red button to disconnect her.

*

It is important to always answer the thing when she phones, in case she takes it upon herself to visit me. Áine's my eldest, she's a divil for interfering, but won't interfere when interfering is necessary.
—Mammy what are you doing on the bus? Áine, back in my ear again. She always sounds impatient with me, even when wishing me Happy Birthday she sounds like she wishes it had less letters.
—Áine I am not on the bus anymore.
—Where are you now?
—I'm with Joanie, I said. I could hear her relax.
—Well, she said, I need to talk to you so you'd better be home later.
—Very good. I said the way her father would have and let my thumb slip again to hit the red button. I love to terminate

a red button. I can't resist it. I've given up offering God Bless the way other mothers do.

*

I don't recall exactly when the Blue House became so important to me. It crept up and took me over in the way projects take me over. I'm in them before I contemplate them.

Our Woman takes the bus.

Too many Prime Time programmes on random gang violence in Limerick have her nervous of car-nappings. She read the word in an article about Brazil, thus Brazil and Limerick have merged. Never mind that legions live a peaceful life there, when they see her Mayo plates they see a plump duck, an invite to attack her. She can see faceless people pulling shovels from the boots of their cars to batter her into the ground, flattening her like a mole.

The bus driver, his stomach pressed against the steering wheel like the pleat of a duvet, explains the estate is on the outskirts. Hard enough to get there by bus, but describes the way to do it and wait now, 'til he sees, can he leave her at this spot, not on his route, but what harm, might it be easier for her, it would, it would so. A ruse to get her to sit up beside him perhaps. He talks of his daughters, one away in London, most unfortunately the other married a farmer in Thurles. And does he like the husband? I do, he says but I didn't want her going marrying this quick, but what can I do? Two hours and Our Woman's learnt of many things he likes and doesn't like, his wife trying to insist he eat salad, he's worried about farming subsidies, people are driving too fast and no offense now, but he doesn't like Enda Kenny. She's no opinion on the man, she says. Whether he eats salad or he doesn't, he has generously delivered her, she's there, stood in front of generic wood door, generic net curtains but peculiar statues stare at her from the window. China mermaids are they? White. An odd white, a not-quite-belonging white. Like they should have a dirty smudge where someone lifted them absentmindedly after messin' with a car.

*

A man, nervous fluster of an aging male, answers.
—Yes.
—Hello.
—What is it?
—I need to talk to you.
—Is it you?
—It is.
—He's long dead your father.
—He is.
—Is there trouble?
—No. No. It's about the house above. I wonder would you rent it to me.
—There's little left of it to rent.
—I'd be happy with what's left.
—What do you want with it? It'd only be good for grazing animals.
—That's all I want it for.
—Call back next week and give me the chance to think.
If all were to be well it should have ended there. But as she's leaving, he calls after her are her family well?
—There's little left of them now. I lost my husband and my son recently as well.
He's sorry. He won't ask her what happened for he wouldn't want to upset her like you know. Confused, he mutters, it'd probably be no harm if she was to have animals in about the place, he hasn't been near it in years. But she better call back for he'd have to think about it. Goodbye now and in he's gone, catching the tail of his dressing gown belt in the door

and struggling before re-opening it. She's careful and doesn't look back. She won't have him embarrassed. She knows what way fellas go when you catch them short. She hears the door slam. It may have lost her the house, the dressing gown belt may have scuppered it.

*

She wanted him to ask what happened. She wanted to be upset by his inquiry after her dead men. What is wrong with her? She'd be happy enough if someone was to take the time to assume they'd upset her by asking the questions she's delighted to answer. I had a husband and a son and they were both taken from me suddenly and what have I learnt from this? I have learned no answers. I've learnt to act rather than wonder. I've learnt only how to misbehave.

*

On the bus back, the wobbly, straw-haired alcoholic the bus driver cautioned them about on the way down, this fella who selects Eastern Europeans to sit beside . . . well here he is now stagger-teetering his way back the bus. Heads are down, clear of his gaze – don't, don't sit beside me, whatever my sins, don't choose me. Plunge, plonk. The smell hits her the way heat swipes your face at the oven door. His heat says drink hath been consumed and will continue to do so as long as there is a pulse left in me. He's a desperate alcoholic, the one who'd see every limb removed before he'd quit. Below the above-the-waist stink of him, he's soiled himself since he stepped off the bus and barely noticed because his inebriation insulates against the embarrassment of the trace of wet on a leg. Even the man's eyebrows are in disarray.

A lean, his nostrils toward her.

—You're going to Dublin, is it?

She nods. (She can't speak to him because he'll talk the

whole way home.) The bus is headed the opposite direction. Should she tell him lightly that he doesn't know whether he's coming or going today? She remembers the earlier refrain, arra he's harmless enough. He can sleep it off instead.

There's plenty harm in the smell of him as the stench now is turning her stomach. The small bangs from his right forearm which falls onto her every time the bus turns. What can she do with it, only shove it off, or lift him up by his sleeve.

Once he's in a deep enough sleep, she's an idea. A handful of baby wipes Joanie tucked into her handbag a while before – did Joanie think diabetes caused dribbling? She goes to work on him. His hands are in awful shape. She wipes one, tentative so he will not wake to see she's repairing his hygiene. Above, she opens the air vent. No effect. She's pegged in by him. He's bitten the corner of his mouth and there are various scars on his face, but his hands are the worst. Swollen with muck and either hard drinking or hard work, his unnaturally widened fingernails and bludgeoned fingers are difficult to improve. He's young enough beneath the damage, yet rolling through bottle to bottle. She could bring him home and fix him up. She could put him in the Blue House.

It's the neglect that grabs her. He reminds her of an injury she once sustained trying to move a lump of rock in the field. It slipped back. An extended moment with her left hand pinned underneath it, a pain that gave way to a numb astonishment. Her screams brought Jimmy and he rolled the rock away. It was only in retreat did the scale of the pain raise itself back to an accurate octave. She remembered her son holding her left hand in his two hands, and pressing it into his armpit to bring the blood back to it and her roaring and him *Mam, mam can you feel your fingers?* and pulling her amid this distraction to the kitchen, him muttering *oh Jesus Christ*.

This fella today is under the rubble that's himself, inebriated against it all, even a strange woman mopping him up on the bus. And what it is to have someone pull at your hand and demand the blood come back to it. What it is. What it is to have someone mutter oh Jesus Christ on your behalf. What it is.

Through the window, she forces her attention onto the landscape in the hope of any explanation that might take her from yet another public dissolve. Long finished, uninhabited developments gouge the edge of the countryside, leaking out from every village with names more redolent of fizzy wines than serious settlements. They infringe where cattle once grazed. Eventually there will be nothing left between villages, no lead into them and no lead out. You don't see people walking so much anymore, she thinks. There's no rhythm to lull you. There's no slow pace of a person headed up the town. The town that's two streets and a crossroads. They say the population is swelling but the roadside is so bereft of people you'd swear they'd been wiped off by an epidemic. The development and its pace are akin to the disgrace of him beside her. Caught up in itself it pays no heed to those wandering among it, just the gallop forward and he, like it, just the daily lift to the lips, never mind where he shits or sleeps or makes a fool of himself.

Yet there's something to admire in all the disgrace of him, that he cares so little, that he's proudly reduced. Were he in her situation he'd act on her desires. Desires that have taken her into this bus to Limerick to knock at the door of a man who has instructed her to return for his verdict. He'd lay his head whereever he has cause or need to and would not go to Limerick to ask permission, nor hesitate asking permission to do this or that. He needs no permission to head to the pub each day and there's no pub would caution him until he started to smash the place up.

She'll do like him. She'll no more wait to enter the Blue House. She'll go back to your man next week to seek his permission to be in a house he doesn't give a toss about because she's committed to do so. She's tired of fellas telling her yes and no. Tomorrow she'll go over to the house and decide on the state of it.

*

The next Thursday she found out how bitter he was. She returned against her better judgment, against instinct, she returned only because he told her to.

—Oh it's you again, he snaps at the door.

—You told me come back.

—Well it's a wasted journey. The place is not for rent. And I'll hear no more about. Don't come bothering me again do ya hear?

Before he can shut the brown door.

—Where was it again you were born, where in the family were you, the youngest or the middle?

—What would you want to know such a thing for?

—You're not the youngest I am certain?

—That I am not. The youngest is gone. Cirrhosis of the liver he had and his own stupidity what gave it to him.

It's just a moment. She stares into that moment. It's interrupted by the clip of the door closing. But he has given her a moment and it means he'll give it again.

Like a mad woman she calls through the letter box.

—I remember your granny at the front of the house. She had something in her hand she was always fixing. Bad tempered she was. I felt sorry for you all.

Silence.

—I don't know why you hold onto such a place if there's nothing good held in it for you.

Silence.

—I could make it nice and then you could come back to it.

The shadow marches back through the glass growing

wider as she lifts her brow away from it. The door's pulled back sudden.

—If you don't move away from my door immediately I'll have you removed. Get gone.

She doesn't move. She examines his blushed red face and unkempt random strips of hair.

—You're awful unfriendly, she states blithely.

—What kind of a lunatic are you? Go home woman and if you cross this path ever again I'll get an order against you.

She moves away. She's light. Whatever it is, he doesn't like meddling women. She's not a bit afraid of him. He reminds her of the man on the bus, only he's upright, but inside, he's as broken as any of them.

Since Jimmy's death she's become more reckless. She says strange things she never would have dared to before. She acts on her impulses. Like now, his wheelie bin is out in the road, probably left there for days. She opens it. Empty. Then wheels it back to the door and knocks. His face is astonished. The kind of astonishment where his arms could take an involuntary swing at her. She doesn't give a hoot.

—Don't leave your wheelie bin out on the road or the lads'll turn it over on you. They're expensive. We don't have them up our way. Take care of it.

Somehow, these sentences and his slamming the door, and her, scuttling away, are in perfect unison, so there is no outright victor. She hears another bang at the end of the path, which suggests he watched her disappear in bewilderment.

On the bus she sleeps. Her face slides and smears the cold window to wake her. The fatigue of what she has to do now, to settle this situation, all is clear to her.

*

That night she is manic with excitement at her performance. I was terrific she thinks. I stood there and I was terrific. To celebrate, in the dark, she makes her way to his house and admires the windows with her torch.

*

In the Blue House today she sits on the low Chinese fabric stool amid the rubble and jumble of the life that departed here so inexplicably that day. Those waves from Jimmy's hand are still with her from the bus and new ones arrive as she sits in the house she is not supposed to be in. Her back is cramped down. She looks at the wall and there's Jimmy now waving back at her. Hello mam, he says, it's not so bad, once you get used to the cold, sure it's not.

—But it is bad, it's awful bad Jimmy. You've no idea how this cold bothers me. I'm freezing all the time, I'm never warm these days Jimmy.

You've to get yourself a continental quilt and stitch it onto yourself now, do ya hear? He calls back and they both laugh. Is it cold there too? She asks him. Ah mam, it's freezing once you're dead, only you are numb and you feel none of it the way you do in life. I miss you so much, she tells him and she lowers her head because of the push of tears.

Then he's gone and the cold damp is down on her. With little left in the way of roof and negligible light, torch and lighter alone, she pulls the blanket round her and cramps the knees into her chest and huddles. If it was light, she could get on with something in here but because it's dark, she'll just sit and when the cold is unbearable, she'll rock a bit. She's glad to be here. Sad and glad, her strange combination.

*

The doctor phones her early.

—Can she come down? He wants to check her blood sugar.

It's most inconvenient for she wants to head to the Blue House first and continue what she commenced yesterday.

EPISODE 14

Nobody understands how tired widows get. At first everyone wants a bit of you. A slice. To peel the skin from the orange. Then slowly they all leave you alone unless say you go mad or get a haircut or something useful. It's easy to forget widows. They illuminate themselves once a year around anniversaries of other people dying. Then people remember they are the remnants of the person who has gone. Often about what's gone are widows, rather than the matter that they are still here.

*

I must appreciate why my daughters were angry with me? Grief said.

I did not.

—You kept the news about Jimmy quiet. Deliberately quiet. And she wondered why I had done that? Why was that?

I didn't like her question. I didn't like her tunnelling into me like that. I thought she'd gone bobbins. I didn't want to tell her the truth I had known long in advance of them telling me he was dead that he was dead and none had believed me.

Grief persists, nudges me a touch.

—I want to know why my daughters are angry, don't I?

This is true, had I maybe asked her the question, had she any idea what made girls so angry the way Áine has gone angry on me. I don't recall if I asked her.

—Have you ever been angry?

—I was angry once I said. I was very angry with my son once.

—And what did you do?

—I worked my hardest to have him go away. To have him out of sight, so I wouldn't have to look at him anymore.

—And that was the only time you were angry?

—No I was angry, particularly angry, twice with my husband. He forced Jimmy outta college, cut him off financially. And he was perhaps unfaithful to me in my marriage.

—And which made me the angrier?

—It was another time that made me angrier it was the day he prevented me from making my son a decent breakfast. The day we went to the funeral and wasn't I racing to be home and have the breakfast made and didn't he take off to Ballina instead of leaving me home and you know how the story went.

—But you too, you wanted Jimmy gone, isn't that right? Why was that?

—You're asking me too many questions I said. You're giving me a headache. I'd like to talk about what was on the telly last night instead.

There was a long silence which I gave in to.

—You've to understand I was telling them long before he was gone that Jimmy was dead. I'd long buried him by the time he died. It was my husband's death that took me by surprise.

—Lookit if I knew why I kept it quiet then I probably would not have kept it quiet at all.

—Right.

—Jimmy and I had an understanding. And in that understanding he wanted me to tell people only when I was ready.

—And how did you know this?

—We've talked about it, I said. Defeated.

—Do you talk to him regularly?

—As a matter of fact I do.

As a matter of fact that was how my husband put me inside the hospital.

As a matter of fact it was.

Did you know that?

Grief shook her head.

—I only know what it is you want to tell me. She replies.

*

As a matter of fact I had had enough of this grief counselling.

As a matter of fact I'd had enough of Grief herself.

As a matter of fact there are a hundred people I would rather talk to.

As a matter of fact.

*

Did I think that the fact I kept their brother's death so quiet might have angered the girls? Grief carried on.

—They were angry long before he died. I left it at that.

She would never understand me that's why I had been sent to see her. They always want you to chat to people who don't understand you otherwise they'd have no job to do. I was sat here doing a favour and a service to this woman, so I was.

A short silence, that should have been a long silence, a very long one, that I should not have given in to.

—Jimmy was everything to me and he left me with the decision about how to tell or say when he was or was not dead. He had told me earlier than the rest of you. We'd talked about it. And even after his death we talked about it. Take your time mam he'd said. I was visiting him up in the Blue House sure.

And it's out of me, and I am looking at it like it's someone else's washing on the line and I have done the very thing I vowed I wouldn't to Bina. I have alarmed Grief and it's a bad turn I have taken.

Sure enough Grief can't see me for a couple of weeks, but she wants me to meet someone else in Castlebar while she is gone and she'll be calling me with an appointment.

*

That extra appointment surged in me the need to inhabit the Blue House because I felt they were coming for me. Simply inhabit to not be here, to not listen to the details of the appointment. I had no strength for listening this day or any day. I wanted only to sit on the small Chinese footstool and talk to Jimmy. He never bothered me with these incessant questions. He only worried about me catching cold. I longed to be back talking to him no matter how uncomfortable the house.

*

There could be no telling me. He was dead and gone and I knew it. No matter what their mouths said back to me. I knew exactly where my son was. He was in the Blue House.

*

It was after that session with Grief that the woman came visiting me at the house. The Outreach Team woman she called herself. Nice enough she was, sporting an emphatic bobbed hairstyle, a shortish round woman. She was friendly and clapped her hands together a lot, as if to say come on now lads, sort it out. Except there were no lads anymore. She would be coming to see me once a week and I was to be going to another clinic every other week. She asked an awful lot of questions I became confused about what I was answering and answered yes to every single one so she would go home and leave me in peace.

This was a bad sign. When they're in your house, they're coming for ya, Bina said.

Bina instructed me firstly not to let her in, then said she'd better move in to be certain they did not take me away.

Be careful Phil, she said, they're comin' for ye.

EPISODE 15

When they came, I'd been expecting them. Knew how they'd look, knew I would know they'd come before they knocked on my door. And I did. The phone rang. Naturally the phone rang. The phone always rings. This is the problem with the phone. I nearly miss the days when we'd to go two and a half miles to the pub and wait out the evening for the pay phone to ring for us, for someone to call out is so and so here: a call from England. And everyone would push out of the way and let you through in a hurry, all hoping the voice would still be there on the line for ya. The miracle of telephony, none of us understanding how it all happened. Nor did we want to, we only wanted the voice to be there. And it was similar when they came to my door to tell me about Jimmy. I only hoped the miracle would be he was still there, but I had known for so much longer than they gave me credit for, that he was not.

*

It was in the hesitant way they unlatched the gate and closed it behind them as if they'd be staying awhile. I had the door open for I would not let them rest their knuckles on it and enjoy that pause before it pulled back. I unlatched it only because if they hadn't delivered the news they'd retire to a

local pub, and two and two would make eight and I wanted
them gone from here with their blue and starched collars. Let
it be in my ear canal rather than the entire village and mostly
I wanted them gone.

—I know why you've come. I've been expecting you. Is it
what I think it is? If it is just nod.

*

They commenced their emotionless speech delivered like
they were brushing their teeth and avoiding the gums. She
let them talk and at the end calmly nodded. She would not
do what she'd heard the mother in Florida did, ran out to the
garden threw herself to the ground, vomited, pulled at clumps
of grass and roared. She would do none of it.

*

—Well you have him now, I said, you have taken all of him
from me and now if you'll excuse me I have chores to attend to.

I closed the door on them and returned to my kitchen table.
I lifted my pen and wrote the number + 1 on the bottom of
the table mat. Then I rose and put the flat of my right hand
onto the hot range and wanted it left there for the count of
four. I wanted to tattoo this moment onto myself. I could not
last 'til four.

Finally after so many months, after administering that burn
to my hand I no longer felt numb.

*

In her mind it was old news, she reminded herself, for she'd
known all this since that time Himself had taken her to the
hospital. She was telling them all that time Jimmy was gone.
She knew that they would take Jimmy from her. And they had
done it. There was nothing new in this, she told herself. She
would not allow for surprise.

What did surprise her was how angry she became at her husband, who by virtue of his own inconvenient death had absented himself from this final chapter. She longed for him to see the results of their enterprise, to see precisely what they'd achieved. She stared at the wall and actively wondered how much more stupid two people could have been.

*

She would tell the world when she was ready. She felt she'd a plan once she closed the door on them. She just could not recall what it was. She sat into the chair and immediately worried about what they had been saying in the bank, that Jimmy had gone to America to be shut of her.

*

Even tho' Jimmy was nowhere near New Jersey she scans every scene of the film for a sighting of him, a boot, an elbow, an eyebrow – that rare remote chance. A television documentary about men waking up in New Jersey on the day they are due to ship out to Iraq surprises her in its timing and she compulsively views it knowing this to be a poor decision. There's women stood among them, women, and not just that shiny-eyed wife she's used to seeing hand over children, forever dressed in snowsuits, to their fathers. Women kiss their husbands goodbye. The men aren't going no place. Women in uniforms with rucksacks about them. Women, she repeats to herself, there were women there for God's sake. Could Jimmy not have tumbled into the arms of some girl? The Lord Save Us to even think such a thought. It broke her out in a reluctant smile. It makes her sad for one reason and it's not goodbye to families. It's that her Jimmy could have found himself a wife. She briefly imagines Jimmy in some kind of a squadron or situation where it's him, only him and thirty-two women in uniforms: she tries to imagine him among them. But he looks

lost and the image of a shirtless male is all she can draw up.
She can see her Jimmy looking at the man's face and body
and shame her as it might, the idea of it breaks her.

She's angry because her tears are interrupting the details
of the documentary and all she's after these days since Jimmy
died is details. If she can pin down the details of his life, there's
more chance she can imagine him alive again. The way the
soldiers are strapped into the stand-up-style plane or helicopter,
the green everything, the Tourettey eyes, the fact they don't
seem too fussed, they're shipping out resigned to what they'll
face. Mostly *they don't know* they say, they speculate but *they don't
know*. They speak acronyms, she notices. She's surprised to see
them stopping in Shannon, staring out the window, no idea
where they are, some just continue to play hand-held games
or they do word search.

And she's back imagining her Jimmy on a similar plane at
Shannon, with his green-trousered brigade leaning against
that window pointing to things. It's fading now. She can see
him pressing his head to the back of the seat, pretending to
know nothing about it, maybe pretending not to be of it at all.

She phones Joanie during the ads of the documentary.
How's she doing there and did she know there were women
over there in the army too? Joanie didn't but sure it doesn't
surprise her. What's she doing? Watching a programme. Does
she need a bit of company? Arra no. Well now. Quietly, it's
about soldiers, yes, going to Iraq. She'll be over to her now,
put the kettle on. If you insist on watching it, you shouldn't
be alone for you'll never sleep after the like of it. When she
replaces the phone, she notices how dirty the head of it is
from the picking up and dropping and means to clean it. She
wonders does Joanie think she's done something she shouldn't
have in watching the programme.

It's with her always nowadays such doubt. She's to tell herself
flat that there's no one can tell her what she can or cannot do.

Just because they may think she's going mad does not mean she's under contract to deliver it up to them.

As Joanie and Our Woman watch together they discuss a few things like the mother of the fella in New Jersey. *The muslin fella* Joanie calls him, mistaking cloth for religion. The mother beside herself, the mother who came from some hot place nearby to Iraq, who waves her finger at the camera and beseeches her long-departed son to stop punishing her. She did not bring him to this country to give him opportunity to have him go back to her land and occupy it.

—I know how she feels, Our Woman says after Joanie remarks on the lovely oak table in the woman's kitchen and the fact she's wearing a very dark shade of nail varnish.

—Isn't it great the women keep themselves looking so well, no matter the stress they're under, Joanie remarks ignoring her.

—I know how she feels, Our Woman repeats. She's this new trick when they talk over her, or by her, they all do it the girls, they mean well but they all do it. Then she breaks down and tells Joanie the truth that it was all her fault for sending Jimmy the adverts. She tells her about college and the fella who visited and Himself whipping the college funds from Jimmy and Joanie's trying to clarify things with her and she's foggy again. Why's Joanie asking is he local? Of course he's not local. She shrieks at her. He's over there, he's over there. He wouldn't a gone near him if he was local. Where would you find the like of him local?

It's all don't upset yourself when she flies into these confusions and shortly the doctor's in the house again and she realizes she'll have to stop telling Joanie anything if it's all going to end in an injection. To think she considered telling her about Beirut.

Blood pressure, hup, hup, hup, hiss. Hiss. Hiss. It's low. Is she dizzy? Has she tested her blood sugar today? Something to help her sleep. He squeezes her hand two times in comfort and she feels like the old woman she is. Old, bereft with people to help her fall asleep.

The sleep is terrible. Hour after hour she wakes. Confused. Things, objects and colours dart in the darkness, whittle their way into and out of shadows and strangely, boxes. The room, the air of it is covered and divided by boxes within which it's all movement, disconcerting movement. Lines, colours dance about. She can see small boxes, things tucking into them and the pulse in her neck twangs like a rubber band and the tightness of her chest frightens her. Up she gets to the light, shuffles into the cold bathroom for a glass of water, she doesn't trust the water, so in to the kitchen for the boiled kettle.

She sits shivering in a cold you would not contemplate stepping out into lest you risk wetting the bed. She considers swapping the night for day to see would it be easier on her. The red light of the electric blanket is hanging down there beneath the old pink undersheet when she's back at the bed. She's tempted to kneel, but what would be the good in kneeling, what did kneeling do 'til now only Jimmy gone and all this disturbance.

She tries to remember a time when there wasn't these interruptions and she can't. The pill, the herbal tea, the Valerian none of it helps. The first time she takes forty-five drops of Valerian she falls down a well all night long. With no cars outside and so quiet, the night is an uncomfortable place to be.

She sticks pictures of soldiers on the inside of her kitchen press doors, believing some of them may have known her Jimmy, one may even have kissed him. There's one of a bunch sitting around drinking coffee and a man with a guitar. She chooses the door with the bad hinge, that dips a little lower than it should. Sticks them with blutack. Every time she needs a cup, he'll look at her. Sometimes she leaves the door open and stares at him while she's stirring a pot or tipping the kettle. His eyes pour out at her, they're the deep brown of conkers and the more she looks at him the more handsome he becomes. They're spoiled really, the lads in all that green camouflage and clippered hair. They've the look of shaved dogs not men. But if you can imagine it all rolled away, all the clip and cap and green just gone, their features come back. He was the sort of fella who probably wore jeans and a burgundy top. She'll think of him in burgundy it's best. She names one of them Raphael and she believes he has known her Jimmy intimately. She can talk to him on the door. His image becomes bolder and bolder until she can visualize him moving about. Once she sees him sitting at her table clutching his knees up to his chest awkwardly. Is he saying anything at all? He's big, Raphael is tall. You're tall you know. I never thought Jimmy would go for one as tall as you, she confides in him. He's a snuffly laugh has Raphael, but they like each other. I can see why Jimmy would like looking at ya, you've lovely warm eyes. That was my problem she tells him, I chose a man who hadn't warm enough eyes. He laughs again and says he's going out the back for a smoke and it's the draft on her ankles that brings her back. The cold around her legs. Stood there with back door open, in the middle of the quiet night and no one to be seen, least alone the fella she's been exchanging laughter with.

*

But she'll continue with it. It's easier, she thinks. If she's to jump up and down and smother every imagined exchange the hours will be so long, alone here in the house. While she's chatting to Raphael for any reason you can choose she's happier and she's learning, albeit imaginary, about her son's life.

*

Beirut, Beirut, the only other thought in her mind, humming over and over like a psalm. Beirut may have seen Jimmy when he went to his daughter's wedding. She longs to talk again with Beirut. She wants to climb inside his coat. She wants to hear the stories of the dogs and the women wearing gold sandals with their good strong legs and clear skin. She wants all of it described all over again. Then maybe she can sleep once more the way she used to. A strange thing is some days she cannot remember whether or not they have buried Jimmy or if he's still on his way home.

*

In Dublin for a day's shopping, the solution her dead husband prescribed. She smiles to think she's begun listening to him now he's passed on. He prompts her to go. Then she hears it, uttered aloud on the bus from Heuston Station, an older woman behind her explaining her daughter, out in Bray, and the council house they've given her, and the state of it, and her daughter up to the counter of the housing office, she told them, she did, she told them straight.

—It's like bleedin' Beirut. I can't live in it.

—Jaysus, back from the lips beside her. Jaysus it's a disgrace. Honest to God.

Our Woman smiles at the reference. Bayroot, Beirut. Which Beirut is it they're talking of? Is it the same Beirut the man in the hospital went to the wedding in? It's not, it's the bombed Beirut. Any Beirut will do. She's obsessed and besotted with a place she can't spell. A place another woman identifies as the crater of the earth. A place that a leaking, run-down damaged council house is compared with. A place she wants to go to without having to get off this bus.

It is after the dullness of Penneys and the buggies banging into her and a look at the duvets downstairs. Duvets, pans and watering cans. All seasons. All leanings. Or maybe it was

Dunnes Stores where she saw the watering can. Gardening implements and underwear they're all melding into one and she's half-hearted in feigning concern over their quality or any desire for them. Picked, turned and merely replaced, her eye on the exit. The heat, the exasperation of shoppers with their hands on hangers and too-short shorts and pneumonia inducing tee-shirts, doughnut rings of flesh bulging from them, squeaking through the rails. Why she is among them she can barely fathom. They might have dead children, especially the Africans. Sure their countries are ravaged with disease and here she is among them. She's careful to smile at the Africans hoping maybe a conversation will emerge, 'til she feels silly for they have their small sons around them and they're buying football strips and socks for them. Too young maybe, she supposes. She could join a Black church, she's seen them advertised. Come up for service once a week and find people who've escaped from massacre and terror. Find the others with dead sons. What's she doing here amongst the swimming towels, finding comfort in the suffering of others. What's wrong with her? Of course there are people here who know death, they're only ten minutes from The Mater hospital, but she's certain none of them, none of the Irish here have lost a son the way her Jimmy's gone. She'd have to go to America or England or up the North to find those mothers. She wonders can anyone here in Penneys right now spell Afghanistan? She probably can't either. She certainly can't visualize exactly where it is. The mad oasis of all those countries beyond Turkey, where no one takes their holidays for Christ's sake. There's none here buying tee-shirts to wear in the West Bank. These countries that are only on the telly because they're having the buildings and bridges bombed out of them. Pakistan, Pakistan, that's the border now, she's calmed by remembering a fact as she sorts through a stack of tea towels that have words sewn on them like "cappuccino" and "Paris Cafe." At the cutlery, was it cutlery? Maybe it was at the vests, the packets of two vests she became confused about Iran – what language do they speak there? Iranian? She can't go on not knowing the answer and she'll have to ask someone here and for fear of doing just that, she leaves past a distracting stand of umbrellas, past two security guards with darker skin and brown eyes too like Halim had and out the closest side door. Would any of them be from Beirut, could you strike a conversation casually and find someone who knows something about over there? Could they tell her whether it is like Beirut inside in the hospital described, all roads that lead to the beach, heavy hot air among the hills.

They are behind her, the two, and she smiles back at them, but they keep coming. *Mrs. Hello. Excuse. Stop.* The tea towels are pressed between her fingers still. *Stop. Please.* Oh Mother of Divine God the cappuccino tea towels are still in her hand. She's distraught at it and heads straight into their arms, handing them over. I'm very sorry. I don't know what happened. I never intended to take them. I was thinking of something and became distracted. Please. He's looking at her, measuring her. *It's OK,* one says to the other. I'll pay for them, but really I don't want them at all I don't even like them. *Go on,* he says, *just be careful the next time. Take a basket in your hands OK.* The other says he'd better search her bag or they'll get in trouble. They push a few bits aside. Take out her book about Beirut and flap through the pages. *You been to Beirut,* he asks her. No, I haven't, but I believe it is a beautiful place. Would you believe me if I told you that was what I was thinking about when I had to leave the shop? Neither of them gave a response. I was upset because I couldn't remember the language they speak in Iran and I am worried there will be a war there. She cannot control the build-up in her eyes and her words sound ridiculous, an old person speaking like a child. I'm sorry, she says. *Just be careful next time.* The humiliation follows her back out the door, people are staring at her. Her cheeks burn, her hands are clammy and she must get to Eason's.

A Traveller woman, a big girl she is, is holding a half-eaten packet of cakes in one hand and two or three children hover near her, tripping over her stout legs. She can feel her move over and see her mouth depress.

—I'm sorry, she starts to tell her, but tears are progressing down one side of her face and the woman God bless her has seen it and stares in for about five seconds, but relieves her of any further answer by approaching a man in brown shoes. She knows he's wearing brown shoes because her head is deliberately lowered. She takes a moment by the wall there leaning in, the pressure below in her bladder mounts. The Traveller has gone to the security guard and she's looking over at her but the security guard is emphatic. He looks over but he has those arms crossed, but he says something and then the girl looks again to her. She has to move off before anyone asks her.

She uses the side trail of her hair to collect the tears. Amazed that you can cry into your hair, if it's of a good enough length. She thinks slowly of the words she'd say if anyone asks her what's wrong with her? She tries to imagine saying it's my son, my son's been killed but it doesn't sound right, my son's been killed and you are all out shopping she wants to say, but corrects herself, she too, is out shopping. We'll always be out shopping she thinks as her tears tumble. Two o'clock in the morning on a Thursday and Henry Street will be throbbing. Even if they cratered it, we'd walk around the edges to get to Roches Stores.

Should Marks and Spencer beckon? That's where women of her age go, but she doesn't want to become calmed by chocolate mousse or pineapple titbits or overpriced melon, so it's along by the jumper shop that is no more, imprinted with For Lease signs and the two brass statues of the women shopping with their bags at their knees. Knees smeared in pigeon shite and stubbed-out fags, but what the hell they're knees nonetheless and she longs to be a woman who sits and talks to another like her about shopping instead of this flustering that's taken her over and has her eyes evacuating themselves in public. She cannot be certain if the grief is worse than the fear of humiliation. She's let herself go, she's let herself go, in public, continuously roil around her head like the belt of a generator. Beirut, Beirut, and you've let yourself go, you daft woman, eventually meet on a loop of Beirut and let go. Beirut and let go.

The Bridge is tricky. The gravitational pull of the crowd is straight over and under like a train through the viaduct to deliver yourself into the devilish palm of Temple Bar. The last time she walked through it she was astonished to see orange apartments and not a single tree. Today there are swarms of hung over young fellas and teenage whizzes who only remind what a great, great teenager Jimmy was compared to them and make everything forty times worse. He wasn't a young lad for hanging about. And the noise of them. Are they worse than the girls she wonders as a girl, half-dressed her bits hanging out of her, races and jumps, straddling a fella, nearly knocking him into her. And the noise that picks up. There's something military about the noise of teenagers, as they spot each other screeching out their targets. It's a strange old language they speak and she's not about to understand it. Would you ever shut up she wants to shout, until it strikes her no, keep going, keep going, keep ramming each other into the wall and smacking each other on the head, do lift up and let out a siren wail at the sight of each other, for one day you might not be here to caper about this way and it's mothers who'll walk these alleys and arches for any smudge that may remain of you.

She'll do the bus stops, waste a bit of time and head back to the station. Up the Quays she forces herself, tempted into a newsagent by the promise of a Club Milk and a paper, but the queue of crisp-buying youngsters feels too long and she's hot, everywhere she goes into she's so hot. They're pulling at chocolate, papers and magazines. And they're all so young again. Everyone is young, everyone is who Jimmy was and who Jimmy couldn't be. She's come to Dublin for the day's shopping to be shut of the voices and the sights and it's back to the Blue House with the gaping hole she'll retreat to early. It's back to the stool and the small hope he'll come again and stare at her from the wall. If she can hear him alone, that would do.

EPISODE 16

She's like a bold teenager out there: the flask jolting her thigh like the accidental budge of a drunk or clumsy lover. Her finger presses hard on the spoon handle. Along she goes merrily. She hasn't thought too much about what she'll do when she gets to the house and she's going along very merrily with the freedom thing until something takes her ankle sharp and fast. She's down. It's wet. This is not good.

The flask has bruised her leg. Hip soaked in a muddy graze. Whatever way she fell or however she slammed, the side of her head – her temple – took a whack that sounded worse than it feels and now she's down here on her side in the dark and the worst of it, is not the difficulty getting up, it's that her plans are slipping away.

Ding! goes the plan to arrange the small footstool, dang! disappears the careful removal of her flask from the bag, and rats! to the gentle twist of the lid, breeze of steam and comfort of her cup of tea, all alone, in another man's house.

She doesn't care about physical collapse, nor cuts, she is stuck and she's not going to be stuck any longer because Lord knows what they'll do if they find her out here, in this condition, with a spoon up her sleeve. They'll commit her, she's sure.

She attempts to thrash her body about a bit, to roll to her knees, but however she fell, something is stuck or gone out of joint. All she can feel is the flask wedged under her thigh and searing pain when she tries to put her arm down to push herself up. The pain is there, no matter what she does with her arm, so clearly it must be broke. She's to go the other way, to get herself over the flask, more pain, it doesn't look good. Dark and marshy where she's fallen, if she can get flat on her back then she can inch her way down the hill she came up perhaps. But what of the boulders, the sharp stones? And there's the wall she climbed over. The wall between herself and her house. The wall between her house and the common land and Limerick's house. Should she call out? No. For she does not want any of them to come and find her.

Of course it's cold, it would be cold, it couldn't be anything other than cold, if you're foolish enough to go out with your spoon and your flask and your plans afloat. There's no foot traffic up here at night. The backs of the farms lead up and out to this common land and it's a great way to access a place discreetly. They'll only be coming up here to dump stuff. Would she be lucky, would this be a night some young hooligan might make a deposit and she could offer him ten Euro if he were to lift her back to her feet, leave her down to the house and say nothing. Fifteen Euro she thinks. A fella would take fifteen. He'd get a few cans, a young fella'd be happy with fifteen. She can think such giddying nonsense because she's afraid. She's afraid she's gone too far now and what was she thinking, scooting back here like a nimble mountain goat looking for a munch. I told you discretion, discretion, she chastises herself.

Beirut is slipping away from me, she thinks. Beirut, Beirut, can you hear me Beirut?

*

Anois, anois, the Blue House with the gaping hole in it. The faded Blue House, her first step towards (Beirut) because she can see and hear Jimmy in there. No one'll believe her, they'll say she's away on the wind, gone with the fairies and ruder besides. But he's there, sometimes he's there and sometimes he's not and when he's not she can feel the cold.

*

—I'm interested in a house, I told Grief on a Friday.
—In what way?
—I want to move into it.
—You want to move?
—Not exactly. I want to move into it.
—I don't quite follow you now. Whose house is this?
—It's belonging to a fella gone to Limerick, years since anyone was in it.
—And do you know this man?
—No.
Grief pauses and then gently explains how with a significant death our minds can become carried away with the urgency to do things – things she stresses that are unachievable and not in our best interests. Might this be one of those things?
—Not at all, I said. This is very achievable. It has already been achieved.
She marked a note on her notepad and I knew I was in trouble again.
—He's given his permission.
—Well that's great then.

*

The conversation is back at me, out here, under the open sky. I believe Limerick intended to give his permission, he was just not certain how to give it. I would hazard a guess that between my asking and his verdict he'd very bad luck with

the horses or a pipe in his house burst, something incidental
to our situation. He was hostile, he was unhelpful and he did
chase me away, but I believe he longed to have me living in
his house. He and I knew it was the best arrangement for
the three of us. You know the way fellas are sometimes, they
don't know what's good for them. It's why there are women
on the planet. It's why they make such a mess of things. Oh
the way they make a mess. It's unparalleled. I can't think
about it now out here, laying here like this in the muck, it'll
only depress me.

*

Obviously I am still stuck out here in the dark and it's not
a great place for me to be and I am not a bit happy about it.
Who'd be happy about being wedged in the muck when you've
only stepped out to pursue your dreams? Honestly, find a man
who is and I'll shake his hand with this broken arm. I've just
remembered the diabetes. I shouldn't be out here with the
diabetes I bet. That'll be another reason they'll squash me if
they catch me. I think I am supposed to push the button with
the diabetes. Did I push the button below in the house? If they
come out with the ambulance I'll be finished. Everyone'll know
and they'll say sure she can't cope. The ambulance came, did
you hear? God love her, she can't cope.

*

If I hadn't believed he wanted me in his house I never would
have gone. I am not a simple woman. I understand complexity.
If the man's face had said no I woulda listened. I took the bus
to find him. His face didn't say no. It said I dun know now.

*

Why had she gone to Limerick at all, why was she there
asking permission about a house the teenagers just delved

into? What is wrong with the aged the way they think and complicate every small thing?

Jimmy and his teenage friends went into the faded Blue House with the gaping hole in it. She remembered how they paid her no heed, and made their own of it, claiming it was comfortable enough. Was that what drew her to it? The knowledge it had been a place her son was comfortable, and when she reflected on their home and those last months – the same could not be said of it.

—But what is it you're doing in there? She would ask Jimmy.

—Ah nothing to speak off. Just hanging about.

*

Nothing to speak of. A leg. Another leg. A lip. A hip. Another's hip. From what she'd seen the day back the field, there was plenty to say of it. Perhaps they do not speak when they're doing it, perhaps that's what Jimmy meant. Wouldn't it hurt tho? she wondered. Maybe that's why they didn't speak when they did it. In case they'd let out a yelp of pain and upset each other. What if one or the other were not enjoying it? Would he call out?

*

Anois, anois, out here tonight in this mud she cannot find the exact story of how she came to know the Blue House. Just as she cannot find the precise blue it used to be.

*

Well that wasted a bit time out here, the remembering is great, but the cold is at me, maybe it's time to call out, even timid. I've accepted I'll be out here the whole night 'til someone figures I'm missing. I've begun thinking about rabbits, they're out here in it too and somehow they live. Oh Jesus now I'm thinking of rats. I hate rats. Are there rats up here? There probably are. And foxes. I don't mind foxes. But I don't like the idea a rat might run across my hair. Now I am really sick worrying. I'll look at the sky to stop thinking about the rats.

*

And so here she is exactly from that thought, her big plan in ruins. Would you credit it? Perhaps there's no getting around these fellas and their permissions. If she comes out of this alive without hypothermia she will:

Empty the hoover bag.

Open a can of sweet corn.

Light a candle.

The vow is made. She can feel how wet her hair is, how the base of her neck, her collar, all of it has absorbed every drop from the soil underneath it. It's starting to itch and she's shivering.

*

The stars are lovely in this part of the world.

There is nothing else to say about the sky.

I have run out on that one very quickly.

I don't know why people talk about the sky and trees in books. I find very little to say about them myself. It's a bit like talking about the wallpaper. They're there. You don't need to remind me.

*

To lessen the despair of being stuck out here among the soggy bog cotton it helps to remember her route over: the broom in the car may have looked suspicious, so dustpan and brush suffice. She does not want to catch the eye of anyone going over to that house. She does not want to give way to questions. She gathers only the critical, the essential, the necessary. Tho' she's long lost her religious belief, tradition hangs onto her by a slight hitch, so a statue and a small square bottle of unopened holy water go into the bag. Superstition: she's not afraid of him who owns the house, she's afeared of those who might be passing. Gurriers tempted to vandalize or the thoughts of a person driving by. Their impulses. They worry her. Someone might choose to batter another, flat like a mole for a few bob. They could choose her because she happened to be there.

*

The house rests two fields over, she'll have several routes to access it. She cannot park the car nearby in case the girls see it. She has to be ever so careful with the girls, if they cop onto her, there will be an almighty row. A widow rummaging about in the dark in another man's house. Imagine! You'd never hear the end of it. She goes on foot and is limited by what she can carry. There's one route, the better route that she cannot take because that's the route she saw Jimmy at Patsy's boy, way the ways back. It helps to think of Beirut and the things he said to me. Did I ever tell you how I met him? Wait now 'til I remember.

*

Balloons at the end of the bed. But they were not his balloons they musta been the previous patient's balloons. Beirut was Helium before he became Beirut. I remember the day he arrived in the ward, the nurse apologizing that the strings on the balloons were tight but with the scissors she'd have them off in a minute. And him pleading that she not take them. She put the scissors through one a them and he let a bellow out of him like a hungry bullock and to calm him the nurse promised she'd let the other alone.

He mustn't a noticed me there watching and hearing for he continued to maintain it was his balloon that his daughter had given to him. I nodded along with him, the way you do, drifting from sleep to Quality Street to injection as you do in

these wards, waiting for visiting hours to come around and
see who would come into you and hoping someone might
and hoping all of them wouldn't come near me at exactly the
same time. If you see what I mean. If it's not possible to be
in two places at the same time, I have discovered it's utterly
possible to be in two separate minds at the same time. Come
here and go away minds.

Helium started to talk to me and I was delighted. He called
across details of his life. A daughter, the daughter who gave
him this balloon he pointed to, is married with children living
up in Ballyvary. Ballyvary, Ballavary, he never seems to stop
saying the word. Up there, he calls it. Over there. *Bela, Belavary.*
Were you ever in Belavary?

*

I wasn't, Our Woman says.

—Were you ever in Beirut? he asked her.

—Were you ever in Beirut? she asked him back.

—It's funny you should say it, he replied. I went to a wedding
in Beirut and you're the only person ever asked me about it.
He uses the word funny thirteen times in relation to Beirut.
Funny place it is, funny people they are, funny food it is too
and very hot. He got a terrible sunburn in Beirut. His brother
died of skin cancer, but the brother was never in Beirut. I was
the only one who went to the wedding. I was the only one
who got a sunburn.

—And who was it married who? She wants to know. There's
a boreen of explanation. A second cousin married some fella
in the UN peacekeepers and the only time off he could manage
was enough time to get married there in Beirut.

She can't believe it.

—I was the only one who went. My wife, God Rest Her,
was terrified of flying. It was only me and it was a funny place.

—My son, she told him, is in the army too.

—Is he married?

—No, he's not.

—My son is in the army, she repeated.

But Helium is only interested in marriage.

—I've four daughters married now, he continued, and every one I've gone to the wedding. There's many of them not getting married these days, he said. I am lucky with my own.

—I've hope for my girls, but my son won't get married, she admitted.

The nurse arrived to check her vitals and passed over to the Helium man's bed whispering something to him. He doesn't mention his children again. They've told him, they've told him, she thought.

—My son, she called over, confident it will annoy the nurses, was a homosexual. They're not the marrying sorts.

—Is that right? he responded politely and wondered whether she thought the weather would hold. It's hard when your children aren't the marrying sort, he added. Very hard on the woman, so it is.

—Oh it is, she agreed.

From then on he was Beirut. Beirut the only person who understood her in here.

*

They sneak conversations across the ward all day long. Usually when the nurses have gone out of the room. This causes friction with another fella on the same side of the ward as Beirut.

*

—D'ya know the women of Beirut take great care of themselves. They wear beautiful shoes. We went out in the street after the wedding. I saw eight shoes that weekend, eight shoes that were sprayed the colour of gold, feet like bullions,

the women. I'd never seen a pair of gold shoes before I went to
Beirut. I tell ya now, you don't see them in Ireland. Here they
are all stuck in boots, old coats on them and their hair blown
sideward by the wind. There's no wind in Beirut, women don't
have to contend with the same physical defeats the Irish do.

—But what about the scarves? The scarves? The women
wear scarves all over them, I said.

—Oh, the scarves, the religious ones is it? No, no not in
Beirut, I didn't see many scarves, them is only on the telly.

—The scarves are to keep the hair out of your eyes when
you're working, I reproached him. You have to keep the wind
back or you'd look a terrible state and you might run into
someone you know on the road and you mightn't want to be
looking that way.

—That's right, they wear the scarves to keep their hair
clean in Beirut, they're very sensible, they don't want the dust
getting at it, Beirut said back to me.

I was distracted by the man beside him, who was listening
over. He indicates his forehead, taps it with his finger, three
times. A bleedin' nutter he's telling me. He makes a curly
motion. Round the bend with his gold-shod women. Those
indicators say.

But Beirut, Beirut was not deterred by his fellow countryman's
opinion on him. And on he went.

—There's no place like it in the world. I should never have
come back.

The head-tappin' neighbour's had enough. He's in.

—I thought you only went there for the weekend. How can
you be attached after only a weekend? Spain's lovely. Were
you ever in Spain?

*

They're both off: the neighbour, he's interrupting. She
wants to hear more, more about the women who attend to

themselves so well. Spain talks on about Spain and Beirut is off again on Beirut. Their voices compete over a woman opposite who the nurses are hoovering something out of with a suction machine behind a pulled curtain. They shout at each other over the noisy machine. Bread, bakery, pan loaf, Spain, weather, bread, pan loaf, bakery.

—The bakeries! I never tasted bread like what I had there. I think Beirut's the best bread in the world.

—Ah here, hold on a minute. There's no bread as good as our bread. A pan loaf. Nothing on earth defeats it. Spain rolls down the top sheet of the bed, like he'll go to war over bread.

Others pick up on the bread talk: batch or pan loaf or Pat The Baker. Wholewheat might be good for you but it gets stuck in the teeth of the quiet man down the end. *It gets stuck in my teeth and it's days to get it out. I can't ate it any more. I haven't the mouth for it,* states another.

But Beirut was adamant.

—No, no. There's no bread in this country only leather it is. I never got a pain in my stomach the whole time I was in Beirut. Beirut puts his fingers in his ears and raises his voice. Repeating I never got a pain in my stomach the whole time I was in Beirut. The women wear golden shoes. I never got a pain . . .

—Tell me again about the hills. She pleads with Beirut. Are they all around you? She wants his attention back to her. And he's off about the hills, painting the panorama, any panorama for she'll take anything he gives her. The arc of any tale can cross this ward and be sucked in by her brain.

Spain predicted a cup of tea was on the way. And Johnny, who was moved yesterday, Johnny is two rooms over, he told everyone. No one answers. One man is stuck on his teeth, Beirut and she are away in the hills. Spain rolls, pulls up the cover and sulks.

—Youse are all nuts in here and I don't know why I am on this ward. I've asked them to move me. I'm going to ask to be moved. I'm moving rooms out of here, away from ye all, he yells. No one hears Spain. Beirut's voice rose.

—Do ya know a strange thing about Beirut, the whole time I was there I never saw a single person moving house. Isn't that strange? You'd expect it you know. They are always moving in Dublin I find. Nobody moves in Beirut. They sit still and look at the hills.

*

The tea lady arrives, everyone is distracted by the number of sugars, the spoon stirs. Only she and Beirut do not take tea.

—Did I ever tell you about the dogs in Beirut? He asks her.

—No, she says, and I'd love to hear about them.

Strangely he never carries on with the dogs. He never tells her anything further about the dogs.

She requests. But he doesn't answer.

—Beirut, she hums out to him, can you hear me at all Beirut?

—I can, he says, arra I can. I can hear you. But he never says any more than the dogs in Beirut aren't like Irish dogs. Their legs are longer.

—Why aren't youse havin' tea? Spain demands.

*

Sometimes at night on the ward when she cannot sleep because Bina insists she is not to be given sleeping pills, she calls out to Beirut. Beirut, are you awake? Tell me more. Sometimes he answers her but usually the nurse comes and asks what's wrong? What has her shouting? Beirut sleeps soundly because he doesn't have Bina waving the hammer at them for him. They're doping Beirut, she thinks. They're trying to kill him. They want to shut him up. They want to shut us all up. They don't want Beirut to tell me the things he's come here to tell me.

*

Apparently they claimed they found her in Beirut's bed. She refuted it.

—A lot of nonsense, she said. I wouldn't get out of the bed and leave my slippers behind. I am careful about my feet. Ask my husband when he comes, he'll tell you how cold my feet get that I couldn't let them escape out of socks and slippers. I never went near him and I don't hear a complaint out of him. Go on and ask him!

Beirut said she never came near him.

They could do nothing about it.

*

She was surprised when Beirut's visitor came. A squat woman, wearing a headscarf, who waves her hands plenty and keeps up a long stream of rabid speculating that bounces wall to wall around the ward. She calls him Martin John* and Our Woman decides it's not a good name for him.

—Oh Martin John, whatever you do don't talk to them, don't get familiar, you're always getting yourself on friendly terms with the wrong types.

She's glancing, his visitor is darting glances across. But Our Woman just smiles and thinks of hills and bakeries and gold-sprayed shoes on the end of sun-tanned feet.

—They've a great colour to them, Beirut calls out ignoring the stream out of his visitor, the women in Beirut because they're not stuck indoors the whole day the way we are.

—Nurse, nurse, nurse. His visitor shrieks. She crosses herself and shrieks again. He's off agin. Nurse could you stop him before he does any more damage to himself. Can you give him

---

*   See Martin John: A footnote novel.

something to stop it? He's off agin on Bayroot. The Lord save us from it. I don't want him goin' on about the wimmin agin.

She's a headscarf tied around her that's slipping and has now sunk to the bottom of her hair. Patches of her hair are thinned and gone. No wonder, Our Woman thinks, no wonder he's gone mad for the women of Beirut, sure look at the state of her. When the visitor finally leaves, Our Woman watches the back of her legs, which are encased into dark, dignified stockings, that don't disguise the angry, bulging veins of her left leg and the drag of that foot. There's something very angry about that foot, Our Woman thinks.

He's very quiet for a while, but the sniffing shows he's upset.

—She doesn't like it when I talk about Beirut. It's why they've put me in here. But I don't understand it, I don't understand it. Are ya a-mother yerself? She doesn't understand. I'd a beautiful time in Beirut, but I am not to talk about it anymore. Would you do that?

—I wouldn't. I would not. My own son was in Afghanistan and if he came back I would stay up for days to hear his stories.

—Is that right? Tell me, tell me everything you know about Afghanistan. Tell me all of it.

—I don't know much, Our Woman says. I don't know anything at all. She breaks off.

—Would he write your son?

—Not really, her voice begins to trail. It's very hard. Sure I've nothing to go on.

Spain, in the next bed, is angry.

—Youse are too lowd. Youse are too fookin lowd.

Spain turns over and pulls his sheet up to his ears.

Our Woman's learnt not to interrupt, just to let Beirut carry on. For if she interrupts he's back to the beginning again, back to the golden shoes and the headscarves. She hopes he'll say something about the vegetables in Beirut or whether they take hoovering seriously.

The only question she asks is does he know anything about Afghanistan?

—I do, he says. The bread is very good there. A flat bread it is. There's a lot of tribal problems. If she's planning a holiday he recommends Beirut.

—Does he know there's a war on there?

—No, I hadn't heard that. It musta started since I am in this place.

—No it's been several years, she says. Since the planes in America. It started after the planes.

—That was a terrible business, he says before raising the perplexing question with her of whether it rains in Beirut. Would you think it rains there? Would ya?

—Arra it must.

—You're right, you're absolutely right. It did rain when I was there, but it's not a rain you'd be disappointed in, the way you would an English or an Irish rain. It's not a rain that would get ya down.

*

My hip is stiff and painful now. I might never get up from here. This could be it. Over and out. It helps to think about Beirut. I'll go back over it again to keep the cold from creeping in on me.

*

Beirut consistently has only the one visitor – a woman – she learns is his mother. The mother keeps her head close to his ear and whispers instructions at him from the moment she arrives to the moment she leaves. He turns away from her on his side and she must bend over him to be heard. Sometimes he lets a bellow out of him and the nurses come running and his mother pleads that they might give him something to send him back to himself. *Send him back to me,* his mother pleads. *He's on about Beirut agin.* On the days the mother visits, he sleeps a great deal and it's very inconvenient for Our Woman who longs for him to tell her of the dogs and daylight of Beirut.

*

They're moving Beirut and Our Woman's distressed. They're moving him she is certain because they do not want her to have the information that he is here to give her. They are moving Beirut to punish her. The way Jimmy was took to punish her. Or was it she gave Jimmy away. Whatever it was it was done to punish her. When they come to take her vitals, she doesn't look at the nurse. Every time they check her, they seem to be extracting information about Beirut. Seep by seep by seep. I won't look at them anymore, she decides, and they'll get nothing from me. When Bina arrives they say Our Woman's *outta sorts* today. Bina winks at her. You're doing great, she says.

*

I only wanted a chat with him and he wouldn't answer. If I went over there at all it was to check he was still breathing. At night the nurses do crossword puzzles. They wouldn't notice if you died sure.

*

Now she'd found Beirut, she was happy to stay. She pleaded that they keep her. I am a danger, she said. I don' know if I am coming or going.

Dispatched home and the girls said it was great to have her back and she looked mighty and a bit of sleep and she'd be grand.

—I want to go back, she said again and again. All the way home.

Bina winked at her. Keep it up, she smiled. It's exactly what they want to hear.

*

I only chat with him. Do you hear me? Beirut I only wanted a chat with you. Just a chat. They made an awful fuss about me and Beirut. It was on account of his mother. They're always moaning about cuts and patients on trolleys. I'll tell them how to fix the healthcare system: leave the likes of me and Beirut to ourselves, never mind your meddling. Leave us on a trolley side by side and let us alone.

*

It was hard to tell was it me or was it Beirut made them nervous? Each time Beirut's mother visited, his situation got worse. It could take me hours to get sense outta him and that's why I shouted at her. Don't let them tell you otherwise, for they will, oh God they will. They have it all typed out. It's inside an envelope. That's what my husband said. Beirut's mother could prosecute me for abuse, he said. I told him go way outta that. I said it was rubbish. He didn't fool me. I saved his life, I thought. You know it, I know it and Beirut knows it.

—You can't prosecute someone for having a chat, I erupted.

—Oh you can, you most certainly can, my husband said. It was then I knew he was madder than I and I should give up the hospital bed and let him into it.

*

Yet when I got outta there I knew I must behave and not alarm my husband the way I had this recent spell. I could sorta see him bewildered by meself and Beirut. It was then I understood Beirut would always be found and I was right, see, here, now, if I'd made it to the Blue House, obviously I woulda found him and not just him, Jimmy besides.

Jimmy knew it, it was why he told me take my own good time to tell of his dying. He knew well I'd be busy looking after Beirut 'til then.

It's beautiful when it all makes sense, so it is. Occasionally it makes sense, just for a moment.

*

My husband did not want me to tell the doctors what I had done that upset me so. He said the stress of my son going to the army was the cause. He said I'd been talking a lot about horses but there was no harm done from it. He wanted to pin it all on Jimmy leaving to the army, when wasn't it he and I who caused him, even forced him to go.

I just ignored Himself and told the hospital all of it so they'd keep me there opposite Beirut. I told them every scrap of it. I told them exactly what I wanted to do with Halim and how I intended to do it. I told them how Halim refused. I told them how I still found a way to go on and do it. I told them I'd do it all again in the morning. They wrote it down. They wrote it down like I was only listing the ingredients on a Kit Kat. Then after me telling them all that, it didn't make them one bit bothered about me in the way I wanted them to be bothered. It provoked the opposite. The worse I behaved the happier they were to send me home. Beirut was impeccable and he got to stay.

*

They're all the same they tell you they want to hear something, then you tell them, their ears fall off and they prostrate themselves onto the floor pleading with you to stop.

Since then I learnt to ask three times if people want to know things. Then I ask a fourth time and warn them of the implications. Then I tell them. I spare them no single detail, no single moment and they grow pale despite their protestations they want to hear. So if I did anything, it was that I simply told Beirut's mother that her every visit was driving him demented and it might be better for the pair of them if she ceased and desisted. I do not remember telling her it might be better for the two of them if she took and died. Neither do I remember offering to shoot her. Though I believe this has been typed up and recorded as coming from my mouth and is inside the envelope.

I could not tell if she did not like it. I was desperate to consult Beirut on two things I needed to know: had he seen any soldiers, any American uniforms in Beirut, might he have seen Jimmy somehow and I wanted his opinion on horses and tried to get it. But his mother pulled the curtain around his bed and if I heard rightly she commenced beating him around the head and I saved his life.

—She's killing him nurse, that witch is in there killing him, she is battering him dead. Shortly after that Beirut was moved again and my wanderings began.

I agree I shrieked. I did shriek alright. You're disturbing the patients and when you disturb the others you go to isolation. But you know they didn't take me. They took Beirut. Then the talk changed to sending me home.

*

A degree of wandering would be essential if I was to find my way to the things I wanted to find. Jimmy. Beirut. The wandering began at Beirut. In those wards that are nothing to boast of, so who wouldn't be wandering in them?

Bread, bread, bread. Beirut, Beirut, Beirut. I told you not to come out here. My hip is grown so stiff I might never move from here again.

EPISODE 17

Arra what about? How long have I lain here? What am I thinking? Has my brain gone on holiday to France? The phone, why the phone of course. The Áine mobile.

To call would be to startle, to text would convey less alarm. But who? Who can be trusted not to serve her up to them in Ballinasloe. There's only Bina. And Bina, who believes everyone is listening to her, has no mobile, but there's her son. There's the son of Bina, the way there's the son of God. Except he's not Bina's son, he's her neighbour's son because Bina said the thought of having children gave her the shivers and she'd never give in to the shivers and anyway the fella beside her, the son of her neighbour, him who she never names, is like a son to her.

We've an understanding, he and I, is all she'll say. The speculation is she buys him drink for his trouble. Bina has taken the pledge. He's drinking for the two of us, is all she'll say. Our Woman texts the son of Bina with her left hand, very difficult in the light and circumstances, grateful for a man held hostage to his thirst.

Stuck in the Get Bina to come up wud ya Hurry now. Good man.

Seven minutes until she has a reply.

Who are the fuc are ya?

Jus get Bina wud ya. In trubl. Urgent. D ya hear?

It's another ten minutes or more. The phone rings and she can hear Bina confused about what to push on the phone and the young fella sayin' *push nuttin jus' speak*. Inhales, exhales, glory be to God and she'll be up and by Christ she'll bring nobody, only this lad here for we'll never hear the end of it and sure we'd never see you agin. It'll be Ballinasloe if this gets out. Put your face down in the mud and don't let your eyes catch the light, Bina says. The phone goes dead.

*

I could not blame my husband the first time he incarcerated me for I was indeed behaving strange. I was up to hijinks with Halim and mebbe it was that sent me tumbling. Himself knew it, I knew it, but he was clever, he tried to get me into that hospital without them knowing it. Except I went ahead and told them.

—My husband saw a young man pulling at himself on my doormat and that is why I am here.

*

He told them I told him that my son was dead, only he wasn't dead.

*

I recall the day my husband came home to find me flying up and down the kitchen. It was a pity. If he'd been out looking for the trailer he never woulda come across me. If it hadn't been raining. But in retrospect he delivered me up to Beirut, the greatest thing any fella did for me.

*

I can trace my first swing to official misbehaviour in the days that followed Halim's issuing of the "you're a dirty old woman" words. I could huff and sigh *oh sure I don't know what came over me,* but I know exactly what came over me, the exhalation of mounting frustration at the peculiar carry on of the two males who were plodding around the circumference of my weekly life – and for that matter, in both cases, with differing levels of enthusiasm, my aging cervix.

The thing people don't realize about patchwork women like me is how given to exasperation we are. On the surface, we fuss over the cleanliness of a work surface, or kitchen counter top, we notice the scum around the bath, we may, the most desperate amongst us, brasso the door handles each week, but do not for a millisecond misbelieve that as we are doing this undulating task we are not awash with rage and salty sentiment the likes of which would sting the eyes out of the most coarse-rumped pig. So this week as I moved through my cleaning I, as usual, lifted the dustpan and brush, noticed the line of grime to the side of the range, wondered how the mounting empire of crumbs and hair and guck held a weekly, uninterrupted meeting between the grooves of Ireland's best-cleaned floor lino, and as I tackled this minor point of kitchen-cleaning philosophy I was lifted and found myself swung to the far end of my kitchen in a gondola-like sweep that I could not explain its deliverance, but deliver it did for my hands were banging the back of the broom on the light switch: it had actually flung me the length of the room. I was also smashing the knuckles on my hand. I put a stop to it, by flinging open the kitchen press and smacking off the hot water and heat. A freezing environment would do more for mental clarity. I threw the brush hard at the window, it cracked, it certainly cracked. I took off one of my socks, draped it on the door handle, took off the other of my socks placed it on the mat, removed my vest and underwear left them in the middle of the kitchen table. I went to bed, naked except for my woollen skirt.

In bed, still naked, except for the skirt, now itching my thighs, I was forced to roll it up to become a thick, bulgy belt. In bed, I considered what had caused this tremendous swing. Was I angry? Indeed I was not. Was it the words *dirty old woman* had caused it? Indeed it was. In bed, I had the thrilling feeling that I was now so old and beyond them, they'd never, none of them, no young buck like Halim, no old relic like my husband, neither catch me, nor understand me. In bed, I shouted aloud *I am not a bit afraid of the lot of ye.* In bed, I yelped to myself (like you'd yelp if you put your hand on something hot, you're so sure in that yelp, the bloody thing, that bloody thing I touched was hot!) *I wouldn't give the rattle of a pan and brush to please any of you. May you all sink into a pot and get heated. Go on boil over. Smear yourselves all over my cooker! I'll never be caught!* I was thrilled. It was a psychological hill and me so far ahead of the pack, the only small trouble was in this bed, at that itchy naked moment, I was headed for a ravine.

Clunk! I hit the tree. I considered the words. Dirty. Old. Woman.

Dirty. Gave little time nor trouble.

Old. Gave grave, wise, wondering, reduced, reducing, stumbling, up, and crinkling and neck and expectation. But all parts still working.

Woman. Gave pointless fact like saying a spanner is round have you noticed?

I had this chat with myself and the roof very loudly, megawatt volume, and it was ever such a comfort. Then the kitchen door handle turned, I increased the volume, *you'll never catch me* I screamed the way a child puts his legs out and flies on a bike down a hill, hands far from his brakes. That was me, screaming and revelling, thrilled, when in walked my husband. I heard him plod his way through the kitchen, without removing his boots.

—Take off your boots, I shouted. No fecking dirty shoes on my carpet!

He appeared at the end of my bed faster than I had calculated he might and I was only just at the word shoes when he interrupted. The divil he was with the interrupting.

—For the love of God woman what are ye at?

I began to exhale a long line of gurgling sounds at him, or so he said. I do not recall them. I could guarantee I was swearing at him. But no, doctor, he later said, not swearing she'd not swear, she is not the type like you know. When pressed he would not tell the doctor the precise words I used, saying only it would flush him red to do so.

*

It was the first time I was removed to Castlebar hospital in my husband's lifetime.

*

I had not planned on it. That's all I can say about that. There was nothing the matter with me. My neighbour Hannah told me that afterwards. There was nothing the matter with you, we all knew it, we knew you weren't mad. It was your husband's fault. He put you in there. There was no need, no need at all. Do ya hear? There was not a thing wrong with you.

If I had my time again I wouldn't a done it to him. And I am out here again. Nothing learnt.

*

I can still recall the drive. My husband tried to talk about the horse. *It's the horse,* he said. You've spent too much time on it. *Thinking about that horse has put you under too much stress,* he said. *You've lost your courage,* he said. *We'll hear no more about that horse.* All the way to Castlebar he didn't speak a word to me and in my mind I ran the word horse and think and horse and thinking and horse and horse and horse, gently to reassure myself that it was a horse that did this to me.

*

Do you know much about Castlebar? I'd say none of you do. You should know there's a weekly newspaper. I realized it once they incarcerated me there, it's the place they want the mad to congregate. In Castlebar they mop us all up.

*

—It was the horse, I told them at the check in.

—It was the horse, I told them the first time they brought me dinner.

—I should not have considered the horse, I told them the first time they handed me the *Happy Days* pills.

—If you'll just co-operate, they replied, you'll feel a great deal better.

—Will I get pudding?

—You'll get pudding.

—Could I have a copy of the *Racing Post?*

My husband had to go and purchase me the paper, the nurse said.

These were some of the new ways I misbehaved once it had been confirmed that I was an old woman. Pudding. The Racing Post. And the hiccups I was plagued with the hiccups.

It wasn't the horse gave me the hiccups that much I know.

*

They didn't keep me long in Castlebar, sure how could they. An isolated incident I told them. They were not satisfied with my explanation. Had I ever had this swing before? No, I said.

But I'd never heard the words DIRTY OLD WOMAN before. Was I concerned about growing old? Not at all, why should I be? But what had prompted this swing? It's ever so simple I said and I let the whole of it gush out of me. My son in a field. I stumbled at the last station of the cross. The spectator, who refused to oblige me, came back and rightly told me what he thought of me once I'd fallen.

Er?

Well it was like this I had to find another way up him, and I did everything I could to achieve it, and you see he enjoyed it, 'til he thought about it and quite right of him he came back and told me exactly what he thought of it and me.

Er?

I took advantage of him while I was measuring the waist of his trousers to take them in. I put my hand down inside them.

Er?

Was I sorry? (Was that their question? Or was it how did I feel? I chose to answer the first.)

Not a bit, I said, should I be?

I figured if I told them this, as a sheep stands on four legs I would never see the daylight again. Only be camped in here eternally opposite Beirut and eventually we would get back to discussing the dogs.

*

It did not work. The talk continued of discharging me. The more I told them the healthier they found me. I was only confused they assured me and it would pass.

After that morning conversation I'd have to do better. They wanted me to be upset about getting old. I must be upset about getting old, I intoned a few times. Then mebbe they'd keep me. Was Beirut upset about getting old? He seemed young to be upset about such a thing, but I thought it's never too early to be getting upset.

I decided to upset them by telling them more on the thing I longed to do to Halim that he wouldn't let me.

They weren't a bit bothered by it. Only wrote it into the envelope and asked how I had planned to do it. I just lifted my fingers at them and gave them the signal. In and up.

—Did he let you?

—Eventually he did, I said. I caught him unawares.

—Did he enjoy it?

—I'd say he did. Very much.

—Did you enjoy it?

—I found it peculiar. It was much harder than it looked watching it up the back field. I was surprised at how far up I had to go.

—Would I do it again?

—Oh God I would, indeed I would.

All into the envelope. And not a bother on them.

*

The second sign that I would be prone to misbehaviour took place in the company of my husband fortunately. I say fortunately because had it taken place in the company of a different man he might not have been so sympathetic and might have delivered me into the Garda van. But my husband thought of the implications.

Another gondola swing, the second one, that ultimately forced him to deliver me this time to Sligo hospital, overtook me in an unfortunate location. Not long after the first swing, like the good man he occasionally was, didn't Himself say a drive out the country would do me the world of good and sure we'd go up to the museum. A place no one who lives in the country would tend to go unless there was someone home visiting and it was raining. It wasn't raining.

A tiny country museum, tucked back in the road that drifted into some kind of heritage land with sculptures. I can tell you nothing else about it. My husband insists to this day it was the sculptures that set me off but I can tell you, and I have my hand across my left breast as I write this, I can tell you honestly, truthfully, I was thinking only of a set of golf clubs when I did it. A set of golf clubs that had knitted covers on their heads. Knitted by the fair hand of a woman I can't name. That kind of knitting, you know an old ball of blue, a dash of pink, the remnants of wool.

I do recall removing my boots, probably enticed by the knitted woollen heads on the clubs. I recall this because the ground was damp and squelchy through my brown tights. The rest of my garments my husband insists I removed while he slipped to the toilet in the Visitors Centre. In removing my other clothes I do not know if the golf clubs came into it.

—I left my wife and went to the toilet doctor, and I came back and found a streaker! This is the way my husband probably had to explain it to them. God love him as they regard him sympathetically with looks that insist how hard this is on him. Stop it! I say. This is the first time his life has ever been interesting – don't you see?

I do not remember being cold. This confuses me. How, if I had no clothes on me at all, do I not remember being cold? I wasn't warm, I was lukewarm. It wasn't a still day, the wind was up, no rain rightly, but not a smidgen of sun. That was the problem we shoulda been nowhere near that place unless it was raining. If it had been raining I instantly woulda known all was not well when my clothes came off. The absence of rain was what caused the trouble.

*

—I didn't notice.

I told the nurse this, as she leant over me to take my blood pressure.

—Isn't it funny a woman wouldn't notice all her clothes gone like that? She patted my arm and told me to take a rest. She called me Mrs, it's charming the way nurses do that, they call you Mrs once you're old. I told you it was occasionally a good thing to be old. The pat and the Mrs.

But they left me into the bed of rest. The bed of rest is where they pinned me 'til I recalled why I didn't feel cold, until I could tell them that I took my clobber off.

—How long has she been this way? Is she herself lately? Any previous episode? All questions addressed to my husband. I wanted to tell them don't ask him! Sure he won't tell you anything! He wouldn't even tell you if the wheel was loose on his trailer! Over here lads! Ask me! Come on! Over here! They don't hear me though I hear him. He was generous, so he was.

—No, doctor. She has never gone this way before. She's a strong, sane woman. Lately though she's been spending time talking to a man about a horse. We are thinking of buying a horse and she's been looking into it. No, the man is not a family friend. A business man. A foreigner, a young fella, a Syrian he thinks.

There! Whamble! He has it! A Syrian has done this to her. A Syrian has driven out of her mind. Them foreigners if we let them near our old ladies, sure the wards start filling up is what my husband is trying to tell them.

But wait now the doctor isn't interested in the Syrian: he's asked for details of my daily life do I work, do I go up and down, do I seem happy?

The only thing that my husband has noticed is I have stopped eating eggs in recent months. And he found it peculiar.

An egg! An egg! Surely to God an egg would fix the woman! An egg would heal this mad equine-concerned woman!

Honestly, like a choir in my head and them all looking at each other and not me and me singing out the answers. Not the egg, not the Syrian, not the weather.

I continued to hear my husband.

—Do I cry often? The doctor asked.

—Never, I tell ya doctor, she is a strong and stable woman. Strong as an ox. She can lift heavier things than meself. It's only since she began talking with that horse fella she went funny.

—Do I cry ever? the doctor asked. Himself nodded. At funerals and once when she could not turn on the bathroom tap.

The doctor wanted very much to know about the bathroom tap. My husband obliged.

—It was a difficult tap, doctor, as God is my judge I coulda cried over it myself some days. I should have repaired it. It was a brute of a tap and I was busy looking for a trailer for the tractor or the car to pull the horse we'd eventually pick up once she had talked to the horse fella, but she never seemed to be finished talking to the horse fella and I'd a lot of trouble getting the right trailer.

The doctor very much wanted to know about the trailer.

—How many trailers had my husband looked at? How many hours a week was he hunting for trailers?

—Seventeen trailers. Not many hours.

How many hours was the patient talking to the Horse Man?

—Not many hours.

But he met all kinds of people looking for the trailer and would you believe in spite of it he never could find a satisfactory trailer. I believe there may not be a satisfactory trailer to be found the length and breadth of this country by God.

Finally there was a pause between them.

My husband filled it.

—The only strange thing I will say about my wife is her feet are always cold. I've never known a woman with feet as cold as hers. All the blood just goes out of them and they're white, pure white and a bit blue even.

The doctor would like to examine the patient alone in the room without the husband present.

I heard my husband, unhappy about this, enquire in what way would this doctor intend to examine his wife, but since the room was spinning, apparently, I ordered him loudly from the room in what was detailed in a report as an aggressive manner including the threat I would put the chair on top of his bullocky head. The deliberate peppering of my language with farming terms was noted as an act of verbal aggression by the student psychiatrist who, later, announced at a group meeting she felt there was tension on the farm.

All of it went into another envelope.

EPISODE 18

Her eldest daughter Áine's on the mobile pacing up and down by the window. Spain is staring at her and Our Woman hates him. He's been filling the ward full of nonsense ever since she went to take a shower. Three days in here, she had to take one. She can tell he was makin' up nonsense. Now they're all lookin' at her.

—You're the worst, she shouts at Spain. You're making everyone in here depressed. I wish to God they'd discharge you.

Her daughter holds the phone away from her ear.

—Mam, stop. Stop would ya. Leave him alone.

—You should kill yourself, she shouts at Spain even louder. I'd hand you the rope! I'd pass you the gun!

She wants to go to isolation.

She's determined.

To get away from Spain.

To be beside Beirut.

Beirut is probably still in isolation. She wonders if he'll mind her broken arm and sprained ankle. How long is it since she was here again? She is confused. How'd she break the arm if she's been in here?

*

Áine's questions arrive like blood sausage on plates for hungry men. Where's she been? Everyone looking for her. Where's she been?

—I was locked in the toilet. I was locked in the toilet and I must have hit my head. She lies tall and proud and left and right and the nurse dare not disagree with her.

—Did she call out? Did she not see the red string? The red string in every toilet to help every woman who falls and knocks her head, did she see it? We've been looking everywhere for you. Even the security guards are on alert. You're causing us trouble, Áine says, as if she works at the hospital.

—I need a little sleep. It's time for a bit of rest.

On cue, on target the nurse offers something to help her fall asleep.

—I'd be very grateful, Our Woman smiles at her. It's been a busy day.

They are charting her when she wakes: Áine is gone, but her coat remains. Áine must be talking to the doctors, which is great she'll insist everything they suggest is a fabrication. Áine will want her to stay here and stay here she will.

EPISODE 19

I had not long put my husband beneath the ground and the first thing I thought to do after handing that holy water baton back to the priest and watching the soil go in on top of him, the first and only thing I could think of was filling up the fields and providing for Jimmy. I had to raise a few cattle, on account of what had happened that day in the car. The day my husband drove the car deliberately in second gear only to annoy me for he knew I had no patience for second.

If only it had been someone more significant than a third cousin we were burying. The public nature of it never agreed with me. It is not the way to be taken, at least Himself was dressed in a suit, begrudgingly, because we had left for the church in some disagreement over Jimmy, who remained behind, still sleeping inside in his room. Himself, unhappy, determined Jimmy should be up, insisted I go in and wake him. But I said let him sleep he was out with his few friends and celebrating that he was home on leave and them all hearing his story of his new life in fatigues and what harm, let the boy rest within. We were late leaving for the funeral on account of me struggling to fasten my husband's tie. He was a broad man my husband, you have to understand, and it made tying ties more work. It takes longer to tie a tie on a

broad man. I'm going to be honest and admit we fought and
bickered the whole way to the church – both of us. There
were good reasons but this was the first time in as many
years that we bickered along such a lengthy stretch of road.
Hedge after hedge, barb after barb he came back at me over
Jimmy. That I had him spoiled. That he was a soft boy. Him
and his fellas. I didn't like the word soft and fellas. He was
driving at something. He was hitting on what had happened
when Jimmy brought that watery fella to stay the weekend
with us, but I thought we were long beyond it since he would
be in a war zone very soon. I don't know why I kept coming
back at him, pleading, yet not giving up, feeding him more
to flare his fire, our last ride should have been quiet, calmed,
it should have been a ride I would fill in the details after and
what might have been said rather than being deafened now
by what was actually said. We did not have time to have that
fight. My husband only had just over an hour left.

Himself had begun his day saying it wasn't necessary for
him to attend this funeral of a third cousin of mine he'd never
met and I could as easy go alone. But no I insisted he, as my
husband, must accompany me, that people might think him ill
if absent and that stung him. He never liked to be considered
incapacitated. If I hadn't heard the death announcement
on the radio the cousin would have passed on without us.
Occasionally you get to know a cousin in their death without
having much knowledge of them in life and I was feeling
terrible on account of it.

I still remember the old red Cortina we drove to it in and
the funny plastic damp smell we could never get shut of round
the gear lever, and how we speculated for years on what had
been spilled there. In the car he was humping angry at leaving
Jimmy behind in the bed. If, he reasoned aloud, he should have
to go, then the same should follow for the Buck, which gave
rise to a rain of criticisms on the Buck. *What was he at with his*

life anyway? I defended him he had gone to college in Dublin hadn't he? He didn't want to hear it, *wasn't he only a waster, a loafer, wasn't there work to be done here, never mind his gallivanting off.* And now I reminded him, sure he's in the military for God's sake – what more do you want? *It's the first useful thing he's done, but he won't last mark my words once they realize the type he is, they'll kick him out and home to us he'll be again. He won't be able to keep that quiet. It's written all over him. Abnormal and you know it.* Then back again how I had him spoiled and he was never useful about the place only spent his day chatting like a woman at the table and getting nothing done, only under your feet and you get nothing done and . . .

I went at him. I went at him in a way I mebbe shouldn't have given it was his last hour and he had the right to be right in it even were he wrong, as wrong as an outdated bus timetable, half removed from the stop.

—Don't be so smug, I said. Newly qualified doctors can be run over by buses, electricians can be injured on their first day there's nothing assured for any of us. He's a lovely decent lad.

—You have made him useless and he's soft every which way as a result. You've done it to him.

—He's not useless, I said. He's loyal. I made him loyal the way his own father was not.

But I noticed the colour in his face rose, the way it went when he was indignant and I thought I saw a bit of blue creep on his lips. The veins, the odd purple one across his cheek seemed more pronounced and when I saw the bit of sweat on his forehead I worried and opened the window. I kept quiet but my head was leaping, leaping with plans.

I knew it. I knew it. He was repelled by Jimmy and it was only me who could provide for him. And that day I knew above everything else I must find a way to get some money, to have money in case Jimmy was in trouble and needing it. His father would do nothing for him, the way he might for the girls.

Then he put the car into second gear to get on my nerves and he drove like a barrel bouncing down the mountain. All the way there, we did not speak, except for a few words that I do regret but at least I told them softly: you're a weak man, I said and I regret the day I put my hand in yours. Confront yourself deeply within. You've destroyed me with your nonsense. And he came back that I was a half-crazy woman who had given him nothing but a bucket of trouble and there wasn't a man in the pub who didn't agree I should have left you and your madness and your carryon. You! he shouted! You are the woman who has been in the hospital let's not forget! And you! I shouted back. Should have occupied the bed beside me at the very same time! For it was you who put me there.

He should have come back with a bigger shout, something deafening. I shoulda opened the door and stormed out, back the road and we never would have made it to the funeral and maybe the day would have been so different. Same outcome, different, somehow different. Perhaps a cup of tea could have been taken instead to calm things down. He did not shout back. He did not speak. I paid attention to how the water flew, leapt outwards from the windscreen. I thought of how much water falls on us and how we might as well be living beneath a waterfall and I wondered was I truly happy in this life I've chosen and decided I probably was not. I have to tell you that because of the circumstances that followed, those were the last significant words my husband spoke to me before what was about to happen. He said I was a half-crazy woman. I said he was a whole-crazy man. What he meant was his son was imbued with the other half of my craziness, but he was polite enough not to say it. He was restrained you see, and I admire him for it now.

At the church, my husband jumped from the car, banged the door in and strode away – his good jacket flapping over to reveal the corner of his shirt had not been tucked in. I thought physically at that moment he was a fine man, who looked well that day in his suit and tie. I hadn't had a thought about him since I came to know Halim for I was always distracted by the darker, younger man's beauty and glow and there was no getting around it, Halim had far better manners than my husband.

—Mind the seat belt, he called back. The seatbelt dropping on the ground and becoming wet bothered him immensely. It bothered him as much as someone being buried bothers me, hence I was dawdling into the church, hoping to hold the person above the ground as long as I could. I had to run to catch up with him because it would look funny us arriving separate and I had to smile twice as hard because he was not responding to anyone who hello'd him. I did not hear a word of that service. They could have been burying anyone. They coulda been burying me.

In the graveyard he was sneaky. He knew how unsettled I am around graves. I'm very unsettled around them. Walked with me and then lingered at the back, touched my arm, whispered he'd to go to Ballina. He'd be back to collect me at the Afters.

—No, I protested, I don't want you to go, I don't want to go to the Afters, I need to go home and make Jimmy his breakfast. See Jimmy was up.

—I need you to bring me home. I need the car to bring me home. But he'd turned on his heel and I didn't like to raise my voice beyond the four cries where I uttered his name and implored him to turn back to me a minute. The crowd now surrounded the grave, I was starting to stand out, shouting at the back of my husband who refused to hear me. Above that grave, as they began to move the coffin, I was crying inconsolably, crying in a way I had never cried, for a cousin I'd no knowledge of. I was crying my loudest howl over my husband's ability to prevent me making the decent breakfast my son deserved this day, that there would be no one in the kitchen when he came out from his bedroom. My third prolonged bout of howling came nearly out of the depths of my groin, I offered it the way we offer prayer, I offered this howling to the misery my husband was going to Ballina this day to reach for the Red Twit. I was crying over that woman lying in the box and weeping gratitude to her for lying there. I could have nearly thanked her for dying and told her the truth that I knew there was only me left to care about my son, that his father had given up on him. I said a louder Amen than those beside me and a man and a woman either side of me, whom I could not name because my eyes were so blurred, linked my arm and handed me tissues. They held me up. Probably thought I was the dead woman's sister. Was it disrespectful to cry about unrelated things at a funeral? I did not doubt that it was. I was crying for my son and for the husband who made me wait fifteen years to marry him and now had given up on us. I had to get myself home to Jimmy urgently that was all I knew.

*

My husband went to his grave in a hurry to get to Ballina to be with Red the Twit and it was the pressure of that hurry and his rebounding thoughts and guilt over Red and I that caused his heart to over pump itself to a sudden, unexpected halt. At least he died with a purpose in his step and an active thought in his mind, rather than say dying lifting up a bucket or moving a gate.

Had he arrived in Ballina and reached her front door, he would have found Red born again to chastity, so better for him not to greet that rejection and then to have come home to me and Jimmy more dejected and angered. He might have attacked Jimmy that night for he was so viciously angry with him that morning, and he was angry with him for reasons the boy could do nothing about. He was angry with him for having the audacity to love a man or several of them. He was angry with me for having the determination to love my son in spite of that audacity. I wanted to tell him at times: do you think this is easy for me? Do you not think a mother has romantic ideas of sending her son into the arms of a woman she can then disagree and fight over her grandchildren and know that her son has married beneath himself and that he'll pride his mother above any woman he ever takes into his bed? Do you not think I have cried while listening to innocuous country music on the radio of rodeo love and knowing that my Jimmy will only have men for company and that his life will be ruined because of it? I have come to terms with it fuelled by the determination to save him from the financial ruin.

That is what I have done about it.

Then to go and die on me. In so public a manner. It was the battering I deserved. I see it now. I walked into the wall that day.

EPISODE 20

Whatever of Bina's promise, her pretend son delivers Our Woman to a different fate. Drops her at the hospital gate, and just before he flees, could she give him a few Euro for petrol? Our Woman would clank him about the head, except she's minus an arm. A concerned citizen of Letterfrack lifted her up, bringing her in to disaster, for – *I found this woman at the gate confused* – when they find you *at the gate* they pay too much attention to you. Precisely what she does not want. Breeze in, get a bandage on it, breeze out, and have the lad wait for you in the car park.

Bina had instructed:

—Give him one Euro.

—the paper.

—tell him don't move!

Our Woman told him, *stay here, don't move*, but watched him disappear, grinding his clutch unhealthy as he departed. The hospital claim she is incoherent. Her story doesn't make sense. They seem convinced her husband or son had beaten her. She insists they are both deceased. No one had beaten her. *Top of her thigh odd place to get a bruise* – the nurse. *You're awful cold, what has you so cold, how long were you outside?* – the doctor. *Do you know where you are?* – unidentified blur of a person.

It is an awful messy show with none of them saying what
the other wanted to hear and it worked out the way these
predicaments do, Our Woman again interned on the ward
protesting there was a young man waiting outside for her and
as soon as he had the packet of cigarettes finished, off into
the dark he would drive. I only need a bandage, Our Woman
proclaims. At least leave me on a trolley like they show on
the news.

*

Bina sits unhappy. She ponders aloud how it all went
wrong, while her biro did a word search. The cover of the
puzzle book showed a woman in a low-cut top who looked like
she'd catch her death wandering in these parts thus adorned.
Our Woman looked at the woman on the puzzle book and
wondered where did she live?

—Lookit, that little fecker I've taken him off his retainer . . .
Bina rattling. I've told him if I ever see him I'll take a stick to
him. What right had he dumping you at the gate like silage.
He's a fucker.

Bina's filthy tongue is up! Our Woman loves it when Bina's
filthy tongue is up. All will be well.

—Honestly they've no respect for nothing anymore. It's the
mobiles and the tee-shirts and the satellites is doing it. You
can't trust any, only your own kind, and even them you can't
trust. You can trust no one do you hear me now?

Bina's talking about Joanie who's over there in deep
conversation with the nurse.

—She's plotting to have you locked up as we speak. Well
I'm not moving, says Bina. If they try to move ya I'll fight
them to the ground. I'd nearly get a gun if it might save ya.

—You'll end up in the bed beside me.

—That's right. I will. We've to be sly about this. You've to
tell that nurse on the QT I'm your sister, any form needing

signing is only to be signed by me. I'll take everything they give me within to Ballina and have my solicitor go over it and see what it is they've planned for you. Don't let them put anything into your mouth unless it's written down.

Bina pauses. Our Woman turns her head over on the pillow.

—And whatever you do let them put nothing up the other end either. That's sometimes how they sneak it into you.

Our Woman has understood she is surrounded by people who long to shove things into her and this will be her fight. Only Bina is aware of the scale of it. Thank Christ for Bina.

—Eat up the Quality Street, Our Woman tells Bina. I hate the sight of them.

*

Bina blames Joanie. She blames Joanie for Our Woman ending up back on the ward. She tells Our Woman Joanie is having too many chats with the nurses and this will encourage them to lock her up. Joanie blames Bina for sitting too long in the chair. Would she not get up and let another sit down? Joanie thinks Bina's greedy eating all Our Woman's Quality Street. As Bina is blaming Joanie, and Joanie is blaming Bina, Our Woman inquires where does Bina think the woman on the front of the puzzle book lives.

—For the love of God, Bina hushes her, don't ask me such a thing, or they'll have the sheets off ya and will put ya in the can. Be quiet, she said. Be quiet so I can hear what your one is gibbering on about over there.

*

I will never know why I returned to Red the Twit for a second audience. It remains the clearest indication I was raving out of my mind during that time, for what woman in her right mind would seek to convene with someone who has warmed the bed with her husband. Honestly, I ask you. Do you know any? I do not.

My second encounter was different. Unannounced, early I landed for I wanted to disrupt her day the way she'd disrupted months of my life. Bonier than I remembered, tobacco clavicle bony, pipettes of smoke sucked in – along with my husband – rather than food. That she might over pull on her tobacco stick, swallow her tongue and choke to death before she could answer the questions I had brought to her.

I gave no explanation at the door, stood silent 'til she admitted me. *She'd be in to me in a minute,* and out for a cigarette she went. Gave me the chance to gander and I saw what I imagined I'd see. As spare as her charm, so her house sat. Evidence of magazines, the holy book, index cards, paper stuck up here and there with instructions to repent. Little in the way of clues to her life, because maybe she didn't have a life beyond the collection and the borrowing of other women's husbands. A pair of shoes dropped by the couch. The heels on them scuffed. Pop socks bunched into their toes.

The furniture old, dank from the days when she smoked indoors. The house, relatively new, but suffocated in the occupant's predictable life of stale work, out to nights of hanging about polished end of the bar, up on her high heels, down on her elbows, the occasional drunk lunging her way. How would my husband have come upon her? She was a *specimen, a specimen* alright.

*

Our Woman can see Red standing outside pubs: her tights wet from the rain, her silly toes poking out in ill fitting footwear, the wind whipping up around her hips in a too-short skirt. Today though Red returns to her living room as though she doesn't quite belong there. Like a displaced object being shoved on the wrong shelf. Nerves at her.

—So Philomena, Red says, can I get you a cup of tea? I am not long out of the bed.

Our Woman does not give explications, nor indications.

—I'd like to know how you came upon my husband? Where did you first meet him?

Red's silent.

What has she to be so silent over?

*

Me thinking.

Her watching.

Her thinking.

Me watching.

Her speaking.

—Do we have to go over this? How will it help?

—Oh it will help me very much. I'd like to know.

—OK, she said and adds more emphasis by squeezing each hand on those smoked-slim hips. Let me think, was it Ballina? No that wasn't it. I think I met him at the nursing home. Yes that was it. Didn't he come to the nursing home?

Red addresses Our Woman as though she too was involved, as though Our Woman dispatched him on his way to her and blessed him as he exited the door.

She's a Twit. Red's a twit. Red the Twit.

—I think he did. Yes that was it.

—Nursing home? What nursing home?

A pub, a sandwich, a stare, an accident – all explanations Our Woman was ready for. The words Nursing Home dial the wrong number. It's the wrong dialect.

—Yes, he called in, inquiring about a place for his elderly mother and I showed him around and gave him our information pack. It's a very good pack like ya know. He asked a few questions and asked if it would be OK for him to come back another time and I said he'd be welcome to call in anytime.

Small dry cough, somewhere around the neck, emitted from Red.

—He began to call regularly. I looked forward to his visits.

Our Widow is astonished.

—A nursing home, Our Woman repeats. And what year was this?

—Let me think now a minute, maybe two years ago this May was when I first set eyes on him. I won't tell you a lie, the first time I set eyes on him I thought him a handsome man and hoped ever so much his mam would move in and die quickly.

—You did?

—Yes you see we need the turnaround on the rooms, but also if they go quick it's easier on the son.

—It is?

—Yes I think I told him this. Maybe that's why he took such a shine to me.

Our Woman notices Red's hymn has switched to him rather than "your husband."

—There was a lovely shade to the colour of his hair. A bit of a peaty shade.

—Are you sure? My husband has very little hair.

—Oh maybe that's right, perhaps he was wearing a hat. And he'd a very nice shirt on him. I remembered being struck by his shirt. So clean.

—And?

—And then I saw him the few times in Ballina. One time he asked would I care to have a drink with him and he talked at length of his mother, and her illness and how much it weighed on him and I was very struck by how dedicated he was to her and I gave him all the advice I had learnt working at the nursing home.

—And he listened?

—Oh he did. He was very attentive your husband. Very concentrated.

Perplexed, Our Woman cannot hide it. Who is this man Red describes?

—I thought him a bachelor. He talked of how he wished he'd found love and children. That the lack of children was the biggest pain of his life.

Our Woman must rise and leave now. She must rise and leave for the recently built front room with the aged furniture and stilted life is beginning to topple her. If she can move to the front door she'll be released.

—Come again, Philomena, come anytime. Red sings. I thought you would have called up before now. Don't leave it so long the next time!

I wish to Christ she'd stop calling me that name, Our Woman yanks the keys from her coat and scrapes her cuticle, slices her wrist in the tug process. Next time she would tell her that he'd died. Today wasn't the day. There was to be more revelations she could tell. Red insists on giving her an awkward square hug that belongs at neither woman. Between them is the crouching shadow of her husband.

*

She must think. Our Woman must think and she must think hard. She must muster that man, her husband of so many years up and back and before her from the grave. She must see him sitting in the chair and at the table. The only place, the only time, the only action where she can see him is at the kitchen table and moving objects. Only in the moving of objects does he live again.

*

If there was Red there were bound to be more? For who would stop at Red. It's in their home, every step he has taken, every hand he has placed is in her home and will be easy found. There will be brochures, there will be information packs, for

he would have recorded these places he was shopping to put
his mother into.

*

Our Woman reflects on his mother. She laughs. She laughs
hard. She was the kind of woman that would never put a foot
in a nursing home.

*

The places she can see her husband:
• at the table.
• shaving in the mirror.
• bending down to pull his wellies on.
• staring and nodding at the cattle market on Tuesday.
• sat in the chair, staring into the distance, the television on,
but he's not watching it.
Did I let him get away or was he already gone? Our Woman
wonders.

*

—There were others.
I don't start easy on Grief. Her face brave but pallid. She's
getting over a cold, she tells me and it knocked her sideways
and how are you?
—There were others.
—There were.
—There were.
—Whatchyamean?
—There were other women.
—Really. She moves the clipboard. To her "I must record
this" knee. She writes. She looks up. She looks tired. She
looks obliged.
—Tell me about the others.
And In Conclusion Grief says sometimes when people die

we can learn the worst about them, but in fact in learning the worst about them and up and blah and up and blah and time's up. I haven't heard much of what she's said. I am still with my husband at the front door, ringing the bell, inquiring, my mother, like you know, is sick and fragile and I'm lookin'. He was gone, Our Woman concludes. Long gone. Gone longer than I could imagine the point at which he left maybe. For it musta been a good while before he rang that bell.

*

Grief is not unhappy as I tell her how ecstatic I am finally to have been accurately identified as a widow.

—It's important to you isn't it Kathleen.

—It is. It's mighty important.

—Why? She wants to know.

I am just after giving her an answer and she's back with another question.

—Because you told me it was important.

She settles her hands, watches me and nods.

—Did I really? Did I really say that? She says.

—Do ya think if you see your child at something you don't want to see you can ever be shut of it? I ask Grief the counsellor.

—Well it depends what they were at and how you felt about what they were doing?

—Let's say you didn't feel good.

—Well now if we don't feel good it's best if we go through it all over again and try to understand why we don't feel good. In fact I'll tell you something, to be free of something you've to get closer to it than you might imagine.

Jesus Janey Jesus Janey.

—But when I was seeing the naked fellas you told me to scrub the floor?

—That's right. I did. And did it work?

—I dunno.

—Are you still seeing naked fellas?

—No.

—Well now.

—I am now seeing half-clothed ones.

—The half clothed ones may need a new approach, she admits. They're a different formation. It would be like trying to move a square to a pyramid.

*

—I've had a change I told Grief in the last session before she turned me over to them.

—That's great. What kind of a change?

—They're not naked anymore the fellas I am seeing.

—OK. Great. This is good.

—No, they've clothes on them.

—Hats and coats is it?

—No, little red underpants.

—Right?

—And I am wrestling with them.

—Whatchya mean?

—You know wrestling.

—Wrestling?

—Yes one at a time.

—And do you like it?

—I do, I assured her, I like it very much indeed. I can't get enough of it. It's keeping me awake all night thinking about it. She grew quiet and then issued some terminal words.

—I am beginning to worry about you, she said.

*

No matter how I explained it to him, Halim did not comprehend the pressure of being a widow.

—You must no longer visit me.

—I will visit you every Sunday.

—You don't understand I am a widow now.

—Yes I do understand. I will visit you every Sunday. I must help you.

*

Now she was a widow Halim could not visit her anymore. It was a simple rule that she respected about widows.

*

Joanie said I was to lock the door. I had to remember. Bina said if I didn't lock the door she'd personally come down here and attack me herself if only to teach me to lock the feckin' thing. Still I didn't lock it. There was no particular reason, other than the matter of them both telling me, I had to let them know just because I was a widow I wouldn't have anyone telling me what to do.

*

Jimmy came home to me in seven boxes. Six small black ones containing his belongings and one containing his body. I allowed the six discreet postal delivery, but his body I met in Dublin. I stepped off the train at Heuston Station wearing my good coat. I walked the length of that platform, absent, because I had walked this platform so many times rehearsing his collection. Remember I had known how he'd come home to me. I shunted between two people with big cases, one minus a wheel, remember I was ahead of them all. They'd tried to send his body to Shannon, but I'd told them no. My son would come home to Dublin. His cremation arranged on arrival. I asked them to deposit the flag that accompanied him, wrapped him like an envelope, into the fire. Mossie at the local funeral home was obliging when I had a quiet word with him. My son will be coming home, I'd appreciate some discretion, it'll be a quiet affair.

*

They asked if I wanted to see him, one last time. I approached, put my hand on the edge of the coffin. We'll only show you his head and shoulders they said. They were gentle whoever they were. He was in a desperate state my Jimmy. On one half of his face especially. His skin was cold, I'd never considered how cold he'd be. Honestly they had pieced him back together and stitched him into his uniform. He wasn't my son in that box, the way they had covered him in cheap purple satin. Take it off, I said. I want to see his hands. They didn't advise it. Get him out of those clothes you have on him. But in his face he was young, that was what struck me the most, how young a man my son was. Nothing could obliterate it.

*

Sand down the windowsill before winter came, did I realize how damp the house was, we're living in a puddle, these were the words that woke me.

I had a terrible time getting up the day I buried my husband. No desire to move from the bed. Granite-limbed, immobile. I felt like a flat battery. Jimmy sat there on the end of the bed and talked out into the damp bedroom air.

—We've to do something about the house, he said, we've to make it comfortable for you through the winter.

—Come on, he said, come on 'til we have the tea now.

The girls were not staying with me and I do not remember why. They were staying with Joanie because they were organizing. Wait now that's it. All the organizing I didn't agree with. But they took it over when I said that cremation could be better than burial, and after that the whole funeral was organized by my daughters.

I didn't move to get outta the bed when Jimmy said come on, but he didn't bother me.

—I'll leave the tea in so, he said.

I could hear the rattling of the kettle beyond in the kitchen, it reassured me if he was to stay all would be well. I had the feeling he would stay, that he would tell the army he'd to stay. Everything in the bedroom was still, the curtains were closed creating a dullness that made all ugly but we'd peace in there, a sad, cold peace. We would not have it once we left. It is this light that sometimes replicates inside the Blue House. The light of sad, cold peace.

—Daddy, I said, he wasn't a bad man, I said, when Jimmy came in with the tea.

—I know, he said. Sure I know. Take your time when you get up, you might be dizzy havin' lain so long. I'm going to heat the pan.

Jimmy was full of useful sayings now and maybe it was the army taught him them, or maybe he always knew them.

Later that day at the funeral I'd no part of because it was relieved of me and wasn't I glad to have it relieved, I was, for I'd a been no use to them only thinking ludicrous things about urns and cremation, as if such a thing were possible, but I remember they didn't lay him out in the house, why was that? My daughters were organizing it all with Joanie and the girls and I think they decided it would be unsettling for me and so into the funeral home in Foxford we went instead.

People flocked to me. I sat on a chair. I didn't stand up. Mossie gave me the chair. There's no need to stand up, Mossie said. At one point the son of a local man who must have worked beyond in the fields with my husband came to me and put his arms around me and sobbed what are we going to do without him? I was squashed beneath him.

Stood about that coffin was a life my husband had been living outside my kitchen, in which he mattered to so many and I had known of it and what harm was it that he left it at the back door when he came in at night. Better he came in. Better he came in to me, I told myself, than not at all. And yet more's the pity he couldn't have made a bit of room for his son, I caught myself thinking. I was disappointed I couldn't escape that last thought. The way it stalked me and staked itself into the ground. Wasn't I weak to let it come to me that way?

Later when all was said and done, I said to Jimmy: Wasn't that something, I said, Daddy, how he mattered to those young fellas you know. Isn't that something? I repeated. Did you see them crying?

—Oh he did, of course he did, Jimmy said. No bitterness, nothing, no more words than were necessary. But we have to get you into bed, Jimmy said, it's been a long day for you.

That someone knew I'd had a long day was something. You see I hadn't really been present that day, I was floating above and around the whole thing, confused. I remember there were a lot of questions, but I never remember answering even one of them.

*

—Age is a great leveller, I told Jimmy on another walk. Daddy for example he's not a bad man. He's a desperate man, yes. But I too have given him the odd sight at despair he mighta been spared.

Jimmy looked at me. He did not believe me. But he kept it to himself, exactly the way I had trained him.

*

Another time when we walked that way we did, Jimmy said to me that he had watched me and had learned different.

—What d'ya mean? I said, not wanting to know at all what he meant.

—I know what it is to love a man and not be loved back.

—Was it the fella you brought down to us that time?

—No, he was the opposite. That's why I brought him see. He was able to love me, I wanted you to see it, but you wouldn't.

—I saw it. I said. I did. But he was awful dull.

—And so you've to stop worrying, he said lightly.

—I'll never stop worrying, I told him. It's why I am here.

I meant it, you know, I meant it in the way I am sitting here now looking out my back window, where it's raining, waiting for the postman to come before I bring the flask of tea up to the Blue House to Jimmy and must be back before the girls descend in on me and start worrying if they don't find me here. The doctor has already phoned, I've to call down to him tomorrow for the new prescription. My floor is washed because I have washed it. It looks well so it does. The cows are already fed. Today I am ahead of meself.

It's beautiful when it all makes sense, so it is. Occasionally it makes sense, just for a moment.

ACKNOWLEDGEMENTS

The references to pink neon signs in Episode 5 refer to a 1997 visual art exhibit called "For Dublin" by Frances Hegarty and Andrew Stones, whose public art installation of neon script quotations from Molly Bloom's soliloquy I remember so fondly.

Malarky is the culmination of ten years' work. During that time many people offered encouragement and afforded me their patient ears despite my undulating despair.

Thank you to my agent Marilyn Biderman, Tara, Dan at Biblioasis and John Metcalf, Juliet Mabey & all at Oneworld for boldly embracing *Malarky*. I gratefully acknowledge the financial support of the Canada Council for the Arts & the BC Arts Council.

My mother Hannah has the best-looking bovines in Co. Mayo and is never short on humour. I thank her for helping me check dialect and place names. I thank my sister for the teabags and plane tickets.

Go raibh mile maith agat go Edel Ní Chonchubhair for translating a few chapters of *Malarky* as Gaeilge.

Thank you also to Helen Potrebenko for writing the novel *Taxi!*, Caroline Adderson, Jenny and Ian, Marina Roy, and Gertrude who told me to imagine an ideal reader. Cathy,

Niamh, Edel, Mary, Ita, Siobhan, Tara, Annabel, Julie, Carol, thank you for all the love and support.

Suzu Matsuda and Larry Cohen, my family here in Vancouver, have helped me in so many ways, including their exquisite love of my son.

Finally thanks and love to my partner Jeremy Isao Speier and my son Cúán Isamu who has rocked my world for the past twelve years. I love you pet. You are the best.

ABOUT THE AUTHOR

Anakana Schofield is an Anglo-Irish writer of fiction, essays, and literary criticism. *Malarky*, her first novel, won the Amazon.ca First Novel Award, was selected as a Barnes & Noble Discover Great New Writers Pick, and was shortlisted for the Ethel Wilson Fiction Prize. It has also been named on sixteen different Best Books of the Year lists.

Leabharlanna Poiblí Chathair Baile Átha Cliath
Dublin City Public Libraries

Praise for *Malarky*

'A caustic, funny and moving fantasia of an Irish mammy going round the bend.'

Emma Donoghue, author of *Room*

'Anakana Schofield is part of a new wave of wonderful Irish fiction – international in scope and electrically alive.'

Colum McCann, author of *Let the Great World Spin*

'A fine book.'

Margaret Atwood, author of *The Handmaid's Tale*

'A word of warning regarding this one of a kind tale of a woman's endeavours to accept the realities of her life on their own terms: mid-guffaw you may find that you've taken it all most intensely to heart. I read *Malarky* over a year ago and Our Woman is still with me, so the process is probably irreversible.'

Helen Oyeyemi, author of *Mr Fox*

'Anakana Schofield is in the ranks of the best . . . Clever, witty, imaginative and intriguing, *Malarky* is a stunning debut from an exceptionally good writer.'

Irish Times

'One of the most compelling and distinctive voices you will hear in fiction this year.'

RTE Guide

'Our woman explodes from the page, taking the reader by the throat.'
Irish Examiner

'The novel's poignancy is matched by its regular comic brilliance.'
Sunday Business Post

'Schofield balances the tragedy and the comedy with aplomb.'
Herald (Dublin)

'Quirky, raucous, and utterly unconventional.'

Reader's Digest

'*Malarky* spins and glitters like a coin flipped in the air – now searingly tragic, now blackly funny. Brilliant, brilliant, brilliant.'

Annabel Lyon, author of *The Golden Mean*

'*Malarky* is a terrific read, a brilliant collision of heartbreak and hilarity written in a voice that somehow seems both feral and perfectly controlled.

Anakana Schofield's Our Woman takes a cool nod at Joyce, then goes her own way in one of the most moving and lyrical debut novels I've read.'
Jess Walter, author of *Beautiful Ruins*

'Good writing and dark wit always excite me and they come together thrillingly in this book. It has a quiet grip on the strangeness of the interior and exterior worlds of love and politics and their inextricability. I delighted in the writing and the scope – macro and microscopic.'
Jenny Diski, author of *What I Don't Know About Animals*

'Delightfully offbeat . . . Schofield shows a deft – and altogether welcome – comic touch . . . One of the season's best reads.'
National Post

'Dead-on, with pitch-perfect speech patterns of rural Ireland . . . Some of this comically laconic dialogue and inner chatter calls to mind the great works of comic absurdity by Flann O'Brien.'
Globe and Mail

'A fascinating voyage into the mind of a woman embattled . . . absolutely beautiful.'
Toronto Star

'This is the story of the teapot-wielding Our Woman: fretful mother, disgruntled farmwife, and – surprisingly late in life – sexual outlaw/ anthropologist. Everything about this primly raunchy, uproarious novel is unexpected – each draught poured from the teapot marks another moment of pure literary audacity.'
Lynn Coady, author of *The Antagonist*

'Hums with electric wit and linguistic daring. The novel traverses darkly comic territory with intelligence and poise, relating the story of an unnamed narrator whose resilience in the face of life's disappointments will stay with readers long after the verbal pyrotechnics have dissipated. Anakana Schofield is a true original, and her novel is a delight.'
Quill & Quire

'We become comfortable saying that there's nothing new, and then something like *Malarky* comes along, which is new and old and different and familiar, but ultimately itself, comfortable in its own skin, wise and smart and crazy-sexy or maybe sexy-crazy.'
Laura Lippman, author of *What the Dead Know*

'A glorious, breathless romp through the mind of an immensely likeable woman.'
Slightly Bookist